LOST IN WORDS

Lost in Words

stories

Ann Calandro

SERVING
HOUSE
BOOKS

Cover art: *Requiem in 18 Notes* by Ann Calandro. First published in *Anastamos Journal,* Spring 2019
Cover design: Jacob Arms

Published by Serving House Books
Lawrence Landing Company
Raleigh, North Carolina 27609
United States of America

www.servinghousebooks.com

Serving House Books is a proud member of

Independent Book Publishers Association
 and
Community of Literary Magazines and Presses

Paperback ISBN: 978-1-947175-70-9

Library of Congress Control Number:
2025932296

SERVING HOUSE BOOKS

ADVANCE PRAISE

Ann Calandro's stories glide from brief dreamlike appreciations of friendships to longer narratives about families. Her sentences are perfection, whether describing fries "crisp on the outside and meltingly soft within" or a survey designed to tell us where we can live in a divided continent. I'm grateful for these reports from a heart "pinioned at the border of memory and desire."

—Carol Sklenicka, author of *Alice Adams: Portrait of a Writer* and *Raymond Carver: A Writer's Life*

"Stories of memorable relationships, magical moments, and surprising endings you will never forget. Ann Calandro is a master story teller."

—Ilene Beckerman, author of *Love, Loss, and What I Wore*

"Ann Calandro's stories lead us from the comfort of realistic details to compelling realms of fantasy."

—Debra Ratner, author of short stories in *The Yale Review, Redbook,* and other journals

In memory of my parents

CONTENTS

ACKNOWLEDGMENTS

Many thanks to my family and friends and to:

Charles McGrath, former fiction editor at *The New Yorker*, who almost certainly does not remember me. He rejected my first short story, "Effects of Stress," with this note: "This one didn't quite make it here, but it came close, and I hope you'll try us again." Those words encouraged me to keep writing.

Sam Stoloff, president and principal, Frances Golden Literary Agency, for reading some of these stories, providing helpful feedback, and suggesting where to submit them.

Serving House Books, for publishing my short story collection.

Literary journals that accepted my work or wrote encouraging rejection responses.

Christine Cote of Shanti Arts, for publishing my three children's books.

The people who read and commented on several of these stories.

People who gave me ideas for stories, generally without knowing that they did so.

And my wonderful grandson, for our conversations on all manner of interesting things.

CREDITS

The following short stories appeared or will appear, in slightly different versions, in the following journals:

2025: "Salvation Salvage," *The Vincent Brothers Review*
November 2024: "Runs Like a Dream,"
  BarBar, volume IV, "Simulacra"
Fall 2022: "Market Day,"
  Superlative—The Literary Journal
Spring 2022: "Album Leaf," *Gargoyle*
February 2022: "The Wanderer Fantasy," *Lit Camp*
Winter 2022: "Sisters," *The Fabulist*
Winter 2021: "Seeing You," *The Plentitudes*
Winter 2021: "Waiting," *Reservoir Road*
Winter 2020: "Longing Time," *Lou Lit*
Fall 2020: "Lemon Meringue and Something Else,"
  Invisible City
Spring 2020: "Apartment for Rent," *The Fabulist*
Fall 2019: "Gridlock," *Constellations*
Fall 2019: "Library Book," *Helen Literary Journal*
Spring 2019: "Refinishing," *Star 82 Journal*
Spring 2019: "Rondo," *Duck Lake Journal*
Fall 2017: "Effects of Stress," *The Hungry Chimera*

LOST IN WORDS

The teenage hostess calls out names in a bored, nasal voice.

"Logan, party of two!"

"Perry, party of six!"

"Osmond, party of three!"

I alternate between watching people walk into the dining room and twisting around in my orange plastic chair to look for Ella and Bill.

"Martinson, party of eight!"

"Baron, party of four!"

"That's us," my husband says. "Let's be seated." He stands up, bows, and extends his hand to me.

"Our name isn't Baron," I say. Sam shrugs.

"It's our name today. I'm so tired of waiting for Ella and Bill. They're always late. Is it her fault or his? I'm bored and tired of waiting for them, so I told the hostess that our name is Baron de Rothschild. She obviously decided it was too many syllables, or maybe we don't look like royalty, or maybe she doesn't know who Baron de Rothschild is. Anyway, for lunch today, we are Baron, party of four. It has a nice ring to it, doesn't it? Come on, let's go in." I sigh, take his hand, and stand up. I'm not sure I remember who Baron de Rothschild is or why Sam picked that name. He probably just likes the sound of it.

Sam is good at making up stories. In the grand arc of Sam's stories, his telling a hostess that our name is Baron de Rothschild is not worth my getting upset about. However, last month, while we were in the city, Sam told a waiter that I was there for last-chance medical treatment that would almost certainly fail, and to take good care of me while he went to get the car. When I returned from the bathroom, I couldn't understand why the waiter wouldn't leave me alone. He hovered nearby, asking if I needed anything, anything at all, when all I wanted was to eat the remains of Sam's bacon cheeseburger in silence. It was only after the waiter brought me a blanket and told me how very sorry he was that I realized Sam had told him some story.

"It's my way of living different lives," Sam said, while I yelled at him in the car. "I miss writing fiction, but I just don't have the energy to sit down and write it anymore."

I told him that I understood, because I do understand, and then I mostly let it go. I'm married to someone who makes up stories. There are worse things. Sometimes the stories are lighthearted and funny. Once, an elderly woman in a too-large coat, standing next to us at the supermarket fish counter, asked for bass, and Sam sang excerpts from Porgy and Bess to her, his hand over his heart. He told her he's an opera student at Juilliard and is making his debut at the Met next fall and won't she come into the city to hear him? She tells him he sings beautifully and promises that she will attend the performance. Sam blows her a kiss and thanks her, and she hugs him before leaving with her fish wrapped in wax paper. Sometimes Sam is annoying, like when he talks to our neighbor's father-in-law for two hours and we miss the bus to the city by three minutes and never get to see the well-reviewed play for which I bought expensive, nonrefundable tickets.

"Fine, today we're the Barons," I say to Sam. I look at him. I know his face by heart. We met in an MFA program, where he wrote short stories and I wrote poems. Our professors told us that we had talent and could possibly look forward to tenure-track positions, maybe even at the same university. After graduation, several prestigious literary journals published Sam's stories, one of which won first place and $3000 in a contest. There was interest and admiration from two university presses, but no contract. There were half a dozen interviews for teaching positions at small colleges, but no job offers. I didn't get any interviews, but a small press published my poems.

"We are impressed by your retelling of fairy tales and myths in a modern voice for the modern age, and we would like to publish your poems," the publisher wrote. I made $27.68 in royalties, and the press went out of business a few months later. My dozen free copies are somewhere in our basement, along with mold and exercise equipment we never use. Now Sam writes marketing materials for an insurance company, and I'm one of two creative directors at a small advertising agency. For years, Sam awakened early to work on his short stories, and I wrote my poems late at night. We sent our writing out, and sometimes his stories and my poems were published, and occasionally he or I won a contest or an award. A few years ago, when Sam was promoted and began supervising four copywriters and four graphic designers, he stopped writing fiction. I wasn't really writing poetry by then anyway, since constantly being asked to write, edit, and proofread projects simultaneously within fifteen minutes had sapped my creative powers and spirit.

"Baron, party of four!" the hostess calls again, her voice aggrieved. "Are you here or what?"

"Let's be seated and get some rolls and coffee while we wait," Sam says to me, and he calls to the hostess that our two friends will be joining us very soon and can the two of us sit down and have some coffee and rolls while we wait for them? Even after so many years in the Northeast, Sam retains his midwestern friendliness. He grew up there. I grew up in the city. I have no vestiges of midwestern friendliness to retain. I ignore the hostess and veer off to the bathroom, where I call Ella, get her voicemail, and leave a message asking where she is. I tell her we're seated at the table. I don't want her asking for us by name, because today our name is apparently Baron.

"You'll see us when you walk in," I say. "Don't be too long. I can't be responsible for my actions if I'm alone with a menu that has macaroni and cheese on it. Please hurry."

Ella is my only friend at the advertising agency. She is the other creative director, but we are really only writers, editors, and proofreaders, a fact of which I was unaware when I accepted the creative director position.

"It's always that way at these small agencies," Ella told me airily when I complained to her. "Only the big ones have separate editing and proofreading departments. We're creative directors in name only." We spend most of each day dodging or appeasing clients, avoiding account executives, and arguing with graphic designers about what clients really want. After all that, it's a wonder we write, edit, or proofread anything.

Because the clients, the account executives, and the graphic designers make the same grammatical and spelling mistakes repeatedly, Ella and I disseminate a monthly cheat sheet to all parties to address their most egregious errors. My current favorite entreaty for the graphic designers is "Do not hyphenate the word 'the.' Please set the word 'the' on one line." Ella's current favorite for the clients is "The word 'emergency' is sufficient. There is no need to describe an emergency as a 'vital, critically important, life-threatening emergency.'" We also battle against the incorrect use of *its* and *it's*, *their* and *there*, and *affect* and *effect*. Nothing we do has much effect, nor does it change anyone's affect from irritation to acceptance, although sometimes "and" replaces "the" as the hyphenated word of the day.

Ella and I calm ourselves each day by talking about food and sharing one small chocolate bar after lunch. We are dieting, Ella because she is marrying Bill in a few months, and I because Ella persuaded me to be her bridesmaid, and the dress she picked for the bridesmaids is tighter and more uncomfortable than anything I have ever worn or will ever wear again. I agreed to be in the wedding party because Ella is smart and funny and persuasive and because I am too old to work at an advertising agency without a friend. Even though I am older than Ella, I feel younger and stupider. Ella helps me with computer problems that I am too weary or resentful to resolve. In return, even though she has a wonderful mother who baked me a lemon meringue pie for my birthday, I remind Ella about practical things, like keeping an umbrella in her car in case it rains and remembering to get gas before the gas gauge is on empty. I don't hold it against Ella that she forgot to bring the pie in from her car until late afternoon. It still tasted pretty good, even though it had solidified in the summer heat, and neither of us got sick after eating it.

I leave the bathroom and join Sam at the table, where he is drinking coffee the way he likes it (light and sweet) and shredding a roll.

"It's Ella," I say.

"It's Ella what?"

"She's the one who makes them late. Clothing, makeup, nail polish, hair. Bill doesn't mind. I asked her once if he minded. She said his mother took hours to get ready to go anywhere, even to the mailbox, so he thinks all women take hours to get ready."

"But it's only us, at a crummy chain restaurant in the suburbs, in the afternoon. Look around."

I look around. I don't see anything or anyone I want to look at, except a plate of leftover macaroni and cheese at the just-vacated table next to us. How can a person walk away from macaroni and cheese? What is wrong with that person?

"I'm going to stand right outside the front door and get some fresh air," I say. I'm tired of listening to the hostess's voice, and I don't want to do something I regret with that macaroni and cheese. I still need to lose six pounds before the wedding so I can fit into the bridesmaid dress.

"I'm sure they'll be here soon. Save me a roll, preferably in its original form, not in bits. And please don't make up any more stories today, OK? Better yet, take a writing course or teach a writing course if you want to make up stories. Join a book group if you want to talk with other readers. Or get back to writing your own short stories. Write at work when you're not busy. I've started doing that. People just think I'm writing tag lines and calls to action when I look busy."

Sam rolls his eyes. "I'm never not busy. Does that scenario really work out for you and your poems?"

"No, of course not," I admit. "You know that everything is a crisis at an ad agency. I'm always getting interrupted for a 'hot item.' I might have the first line of a dozen poems. I thought insurance companies were maybe more organized than ad agencies?" Sam shakes his head no. "But either way," I continue, "the Baron story is enough for today. Look, I really appreciate that you put up with these lunches. I know Bill and you don't have anything in common except that you are both married to perfect women, but you're able to talk to anyone, right? Whether we're on vacation or at the grocery store, you can talk to a dozen strangers, and they and you love it."

"You're right. I got carried away with the Baron joke. I won't make up any more stories today. I'll just engage in scintillating conversation with wooden Bill. We need more rolls." Sam waves the waitress over as I walk away. "And I wasn't talking to our neighbor's father-in-law," he calls after me. "He was talking to me. I was listening. He was complaining about his daughter and son-in-law."

When I step outside to the parking lot, I see Ella and Bill walking toward me.

"Hey!" I call, waving.

"Hey, yourself," Ella says. She is wearing a flouncy flowered dress that would not look out of place at the Kentucky Derby. "I'm so sorry we're late! The oldest cat escaped out the window with the broken screen, and we couldn't find her for hours, and after we found her we realized we need gas, and then I dropped my bracelet at the gas station and stepped on it, and the clasp got messed up, so Bill asked the gas station attendant for pliers and twisted it back into shape. See?" Ella holds out her arm, and I look at her bracelet. It looks the same as it always does. "But now we're here and I'm so hungry! Let's go in and order something good."

Bill smiles steadily while Ella talks. He never says much. I'm not sure why she's marrying him except that she is strong-willed and he is deferential. I know she must have other reasons, but she hasn't shared them with me. I can't remember what Bill looks like unless he is standing in front of me and I'm looking right at him, and even then I'd be hard pressed to describe him. I don't think I'll ever include him in a poem, not that I have high hopes of writing a poem anytime soon.

Ella and Bill follow me to our table, where Sam is sitting behind a new basket of rolls. Two waitresses and a waiter stand next to our table, smiling.

"Welcome to the restaurant! Here are the menus!"

"What a beautiful dress!" one waitress adds, pulling out a chair for Ella, who accepts it as her due and sinks gracefully into it, smoothing the pleats over her knees.

"Thank you," Ella says. "It's so nice of you to say that!"

We look at the menus quickly and place our orders. Almost everything is high fat, high calorie, high salt, and fried. When Ella and I began dieting for her wedding, we agreed that one day a week we could eat a small portion of anything reasonable that we wanted, like two graham crackers, a handful of animal crackers, or one scoop of low-fat ice cream. When I hear Ella order bacon and fried eggs with hash browns, cornbread, and biscuits, I realize that right now is this week's free-pass day, but amplified. In the spirit of solidarity, I order biscuits and cornbread with my poached eggs. The waitress is not sure the kitchen can poach eggs, so I say soft boiled is fine. The waitress sighs. "I'm not sure they can do soft boiled either," she says.

"Fried is fine," I say. I tried. I tried to be mindful. It didn't work.

"And extra butter and jam for everyone," Ella says sweetly. The waitress nods and smiles.

"Absolutely! I'll be right back with your food!" she says.

We unroll the silverware from our napkins, and Ella calls after the waitress to please bring her a knife. "It's missing," she says. The waitress does not bring Ella a knife when she brings the food, so I share my knife with Ella. We pass it back and forth as we slather butter and jam on our cornbread and biscuits.

"This is so wonderful after yesterday's one-slice turkey sandwich with wilted lettuce on dry bread," I say, cramming a salty, buttery, jammy biscuit into my mouth. Ella doesn't answer. Her eyes are closed as she devours two squares of cornbread with jam and butter oozing from the middle. The waitress stands near our table, arms crossed, eyes darting back and forth between us, finally resting on Ella.

"Can I get you more water? More coffee? More cornbread?" she asks.

Ella opens her eyes. "Just a knife, please."

The waitress mumbles something, leaves, comes back, and takes up her position alongside the table, now joined by the other waitress and the waiter. She does not bring a knife. I slide my knife over to Ella.

"Just keep it," I say. "They're probably having some dishwasher malfunction. It's fine. I'll use Sam's."

We eat. We eat more. We drink coffee. We drink more coffee. Ella and I scoop up the last bits of jam from their little plastic tubs with our index fingers. We tap our fingers on the greasy crumbs and shovel them into our mouths. We lean back and sigh, eyes half closed, while Sam and Bill talk in staccato bursts about their cars, move on to sports and movies, and finally taper off to the occasional "Well, that's good" or "That sounds about right" comment. Ella talks about wedding cake choices and what entrees to choose for the wedding dinner. I mention that Sam and I heard a piano quartet at the university and that both the pianist and the cellist were phenomenal.

Conversation stalls. I find these lunch quartets less enjoyable than piano quartets, a fact I confirm for myself whenever Sam and I have lunch with Ella and Bill. I have more fun being Ella's friend at work. However, Ella thinks Bill needs more friends and more social interaction, and I need Ella to be my friend, and that is why we have these lunch dates.

"Bill's shy," Ella told me. "It's good for him to talk to other couples. Sam and you are a good influence." I don't see how or why she has concluded that. Sam agrees to these lunches because he likes to talk. Bill agrees to these lunches because he does whatever Ella tells him to do. I'm not sure any of this is the way I want to spend a weekend afternoon, but there are very few days when I feel I'm doing what I want to do. I wish I could build a time machine and transport myself back to childhood to start my life again. Maybe I would pay more attention in math class the second time around. Now, I can't seem to write a poem about a time machine, let alone build one. How did I end up here, in this place, in this life, writing copy for direct-to-consumer advertising about the treatment journeys of patients with autoimmune disorders? I was going to be a poet, moving from graduate school to prize-winning book tour to teaching while writing beautiful poems. What happened? What wrong turn did I make to get so lost?

Now that the biscuits and cornbread have been reduced to yellow dust and I have eaten the last squiggles of jam, I'm ready to call it a day. No one is talking. Sam sips his coffee. Ella puts on lipstick slowly and carefully. Bill looks at his phone.

"What do you say we get going?" I say to Sam while I step hard on his foot under the table. He drinks too much coffee, and none of it is decaf.

"One more cup of coffee for me, and then I'm good to go," he says.

"One more cup of coffee 'fore I go...." croons Ella.

"You drink too much coffee, " I say to Sam.

"We should get going too," says Ella, putting away her lipstick and standing up. "Come on, Bill, honey. We need to stop at the market for cat food." Bill stands up.

"If Ella says it's time for us to go, then it's time for us to go," he says.

"We'll leave too. I don't really need this last cup of coffee," Sam decides. "We'll walk out with you." He counts out money for the tip and grabs the bill.

"Our treat this time," he says. "You can treat next time."

"OK," Bill says. "Thanks." We all know that Sam and I always pay, but it doesn't matter. We have more money than Ella and Bill do, and I'm glad that Sam and I can be generous.

While Sam pays the bill, Ella and I stand outside the restaurant. When Sam and Bill join us, Sam is carrying a bag, which he gives to Ella with a bow.

"You didn't have to buy anything for me! You treated us!"

"I didn't buy anything. The waitress gave me a few extra biscuits to give to you. She said to give them to the pretty lady in the pretty flowered dress. That would be you."

"That's so nice of her! They seemed really solicitous of me. It was just so weird how they wouldn't bring me a knife, though." I'm wondering why no one offered me an extra bag of biscuits. I look down at my faded jeans and sneakers. Why am I wearing a tee shirt with a paint stain? Maybe I should start paying more attention to my clothing choices on the weekends, but having to look and act young and stylish for clients during the week has taken its toll on me.

"Um," says Sam. "I think I know the reason they gave you extra biscuits."

"What's the reason?" asks Ella, reaching into the bag and pulling out a biscuit "These biscuits are so good!" She takes a bite and then another bite. "Want one?" she asks me. I shake my head no. I need to get back on the diet right now.

"I told the waitress this was your first meal at a restaurant in five years because you just got out of prison."

"Prison?"

"Yes. It makes sense to me that if you were in prison, you would look forward to a restaurant meal, especially at a restaurant that serves greasy comfort foods. But I'm sorry about the knife! I didn't say you were in prison for a violent crime. It could have been for money laundering or something else white collar. But I guess they were worried you'd attack them."

"Me? Attack a waitress? With a butter knife?"

"You told me you weren't going to make up any more stories today!" I say to Sam.

"I did say that, didn't I," he says. "I'm really sorry. I just can't help myself."

"Apologize to Ella, not to me!"

"Ella, I'm so sorry," Sam says. "It's just this habit I have. I like to make up stories. You know I used to write short stories. Now I make up and tell short stories. It's like an oral storytelling tradition. I don't mean any harm."

Ella shakes her head and sighs. "I'll see you at work on Monday," she says to me, and Bill and she start walking to their car.

"It's just something I do to make our life more interesting," Sam tells me.

"If you think our life is so uninteresting, then we should try to change our life, not invent stories about other people's lives," I say. We have had this conversation many times during the past two decades, after bad days at work, or when we look at the property tax bill, or when we miss the city where we met, or when we are on vacation someplace less crowded and less complicated and Sam decides we must move there. He talks to people and writes for relocation guides, sends e-mails to local realtors and gets excited when they send listings, and applies for jobs, but it doesn't lead anywhere. No employer from these faraway places is interested. Neither of us can get from this place to another place, except in a story or a poem. We create wonderful narratives when we are lost in words, emerging flushed and victorious from thickets of simile and metaphor.

"Jobs," Sam reminds me. "The jobs are here. Where else are we going to find jobs that pay this well and have good benefits and have some relationship to our English degrees? What else can we do? I can't become an accountant or a neurosurgeon or a condo developer just because I want to live somewhere else. I see numbers and my vision blurs. I'm a writer. I write. I'm just writing the wrong things, because those are the things I'm paid to write, and I need to earn a living. Isn't it exactly the same for you?"

I don't have to answer Sam. He knows the answer. I start walking toward our car. I hear his steps behind me.

Ella and I remain friends at work, although the lunch quartets cease immediately without any discussion. With great difficulty, I lose the last few pounds I need to lose to fit into my bridesmaid dress, according to my scale on the morning of the wedding. It is a lovely wedding, and everyone smiles and cries and eats and drinks too much. My dress is very uncomfortable. Bill and Ella drive down south for their honeymoon. She comes back with stories of better food, warmer weather, cheaper prices, and courteous people, not to mention lower taxes.

"I'd like to live down south if I can find a job there," she says. "Or if Bill can find a job. We're going to start sending out our resumes. Everything costs less there, even if salaries are lower. And macaroni and cheese is considered a vegetable down South. Isn't that sweet?" I must look alarmed, because she adds, "Don't worry!

We're not moving right away. We need to save up as much money as possible before we go."

Shortly after that conversation the entire advertising agency is laid off because our biggest client chooses another agency to promote the treatment journey for its just-launched drug. Ella and I find new jobs without too much difficulty because we are each other's stellar references, and over the next few years we stay in touch constantly, then sporadically, and then not at all. A year or two after that I receive a postcard from Ella. There's a picture of a beach on the front and a few sentences in purple ink on the back.

"Hey, girl!" the card begins. "Bill and I finally did move down south, but then things didn't work out, so we split up. He moved back north and met someone else, and I'm living here with a really nice guy named Connor. We're talking about getting married, once his divorce goes through. Sam and you should come visit us sometime. We can eat fried macaroni and cheese (!!!) and go to the beach! How are you doing? XOXOXO!"

I turn the card over several times. Why does Ella think I want to go to the beach? I don't remember that we ever talked about swimming, and neither of us likes to get too much sun. There's no return address, so I'm not sure how I can write back, let alone come visit. It doesn't matter, because I don't have an answer to Ella's question about how I'm doing, except to say that Sam still makes up wonderful stories about other people's lives, and he and I still stumble along in our own shared life, working longer hours and explaining to more people that grammar, spelling, and punctuation matter. Sometimes people listen. Mostly they don't. Sometimes they're grateful. Mostly they're not.

"Why don't you at least write down the stories you make up?" I ask Sam late one evening. We are sitting on our deck, half dozing, too cold and tired to go inside and go to bed. I touch his cheek. "Then you can submit them somewhere. You can be rediscovered! Dictate them to me and I'll write them down. I'll even proofread them." He shrugs.

"It doesn't matter," he says. "It's not like grad school, when writing was a door to our dreams. Writing was supposed to take us somewhere. Now writing feels like being in a maze. Round and round we go, with no way out. It's easier to let a story fly through the air and not worry about where it lands. I think I need a nonverbal hobby to balance all the horrible hours at work. Does that make sense?"

"Sure," I say. "That's why I like cooking. It's wonderful to stir soup for fifteen minutes. It doesn't talk back."

Sam leans over and puts his head on my shoulder. He smells the same as ever. His hair is still thick and curly, although now it is more gray than brown. Soon he is snoring softly. We sit there. There is nothing objectively wrong with our life. We have good jobs with good-enough salaries and health benefits, a nice house, and each other, although I really miss working with Ella. It's just that somehow we've wandered so far away from our youthful dreams, step by step and word by word. I gently twirl my fingers through his hair, teasing out the curls, while the wind whispers its suggestions to me.

"What?" Sam mumbles. "Did you say something?"

"No," I say. "You must be dreaming. Go back to sleep." I want him to be quiet. I want to listen to the wind.

Salvation Salvage

Thursday mornings I pick through half-price dented soup cans at Salvation Salvage. Outside is unrelenting summer in this city that straddles the South and the Midwest, but the store is cool enough. I am glad to be here, searching for weekly bargains. I button my cardigan and rub my hands, more with anticipation than cold, and return to examining the choices. Here is lentil soup, to which I will add slices of potato and onion. Here is split pea soup, to which I will add rice and carrot coins. Potatoes and rice cost little enough that we always have them in the cupboard, and there is always a carrot or an onion to be found. I put four cans of lentil and four cans of split pea in my basket. The young man near me is also choosing soup. I have seen him before on Thursdays. He is too thin and always looks tired. At first, he does not notice that I am watching, wondering if I should invite him for Sabbath dinner tomorrow. How can I ask a stranger to dinner? How else will Johanna meet a young man?

"I don't want to meet anyone, Mother," Johanna said this morning, pushing her chair back from the kitchen table so hard it almost tumbled over. "I want to finish school and find a job as a teacher. Papa doesn't bother me about meeting someone. Why do you? Please leave me alone." She pushed her chair back against the table and walked slowly from the kitchen. I watched the leftover milk in her cereal bowl judder before I poured it into my tea cup and drank. "Papa doesn't bother anyone about anything," I muttered to myself. "He eats food that I cook and sits in his armchair all day, listening to classical music on his radio and working on his masterpiece."

As the young man puts several cans of soup into his basket, I deliberately drop two of my soup cans and exclaim, "Oh no!" He turns toward me and walks over.

"Here," he says gently, picking up the cans and putting them back in my basket. "No harm done. Are you sure you can carry all this?"

"Thank you, yes" I say. "I am very strong." It is true.

As he turns to go, I say, "Would you like to come to dinner tomorrow night? Nothing fancy, of course. Soup, bread, a little fruit for dessert." I will stop at the corner bakery for challah and day-old corn rye and at the greengrocer for overripe fruit. The corn rye can be toasted, and the fruit can be cut up into fruit salad.

"Or do you already have plans for dinner? Is your family expecting you?" I can't stop chattering. He looks surprised.

"No," he says. "I don't have plans. No one is expecting me. I would like to come for dinner tomorrow." I tell him where we live and that we will eat at six o'clock. He nods courteously.

"I'll be there," he says. "Thank you." He nods his head again and makes his way toward the cashier. I stay behind, running my hand over the cans of soup and wondering what I have done. But how else will my quiet daughter, who finds it hard to breathe in this city's humid air, who wears thrift-shop dresses with frayed hems, meet a handsome young man?

Pushing my shopping cart toward home, I stop at the corner bakery and point to a day-old corn rye. "That one, please. Sliced." The old woman behind the counter feeds the bread through the ancient slicer and slides the loaf into a greased white bag. She holds out the heel to me. I take it and pop it into my mouth.

"Anything else?" she asks.

"A challah please, also sliced. What else can I have at half-price?"

She points to a single honey cake in the corner of the bakery case, shadowy and slumped behind today's upright cherry babka.

"Yes. The honey cake too, please."

At the greengrocer I buy overripe pears and plums to stew. On a slice of honey cake topped with a little sour cream, the stewed fruit will be dessert. Challah and toasted slices of corn rye will accompany the soup. I head home. If I knock, no one will hear. Johanna is at school, and Gustav, my husband, is upstairs in his armchair, eyes closed, head thrown back, listening to or composing music. I used to like that he is named for Gustav Mahler. "You are destined for greatness," I told him often. I put my bags down on the stoop and fumble for my keys. In the kitchen, I unpack the food and put it away. I am a little tired. I will sit a little and close my eyes, and then I will stew the fruit. I put the kettle on to boil. I will drink a cup of tea with a little honey. Honey was the color of my mother's hair. It is the color of my hair. I have her round face. Johanna has her father's narrow face and dark unruly curls The young man at Salvation Salvage also has dark unruly hair.

"Be a good girl, my darling," my mother whispered that morning, cupping my face between her hands. "You are going on a train journey with other girls and boys, but I will see you again very soon." When I reached up to touch her hair, she caught my hand and kissed it. I never saw my mother again. Later, in London, I found the photograph of my mother and father. She had tucked it in the bottom of my knapsack, under my nightgown.

"I'm home, Gustav," I call upstairs. The radio clicks off. "I'll call when dinner is ready." The radio clicks on.

"A young man is coming tonight for dinner," I say at breakfast Friday morning. Johanna looks up and then continues eating her cereal. When she is done, she brings her bowl and spoon to the sink.

"I'm going to school now," she says. "Then I will come home. I can help you make the dinner, if you like." She gets her books and walks slowly to the door.

"What do you think inviting this young man for dinner will accomplish?" Gustav asks me. I startle at his voice. We don't talk much anymore. When we met in London, after the *Kindertransport* and the foster homes, we were eighteen. We talked only about the future and never about the past: where we would go after we married, what we would become, the life we would have, the names for our children. Gustav had been a child prodigy in Germany. As a teenager he had already received notice for his compositions. We would leave London and never return to Europe. In America, he would perform, teach, and compose music. I would become a children's librarian. My mother was a children's librarian. She read to me each evening within the charmed circle of her arms.

"In America, we will make a safe and happy life for our children and ourselves," Gustav and I vowed. When we first came here, Gustav taught viola and auditioned to perform in the city's orchestra. Now that his injured hand makes teaching impossible and playing difficult, he listens to music and tries to compose his concerto. He comes down for meals each day and to our bedroom each night. Whenever Johanna needs help with schoolwork, he helps. If I cannot lift one thing or reach another, he helps me. Otherwise, he sits upstairs, head back, eyes shut, music unspooling from the radio. He is Gustav, but not my old Gustav. Perhaps I am not his old Hannah. I used to tell him what books I would read to our children and to the circles of children around me in the library. Back then I smiled more, laughed more, dreamed more. Now, with Johanna's tuition and without Gustav's salary, I circle this city like a hawk for sales and bargains. Right now there is no time for my dreams. Johanna is eighteen years old, with weak lungs made worse in this city's humid air, and Gustav and I do not talk about the miscarriages. We do not talk about Gustav's injured hand, because the doctors here said it cannot be repaired enough to let him play the viola professionally. We are here, and this is our life. I don't know what to do except to find a nice young man for Johanna to marry.

"At the very least, tonight we will have a pleasant conversation with a nice young man," I tell Gustav. "It is just the three of us here, long day after long day, you with your music, Johanna with her school, me with the shopping and keeping track of things. Tonight is for company and conversation. I'm not expecting anything more. But maybe, just maybe, this young man could like our Johanna, and she could like him, and then who knows what might happen? They could become friends. They could even fall in love and marry. And even if nothing else happens, we will enjoy soup and bread and honey cake with stewed fruit for dessert. It is Sabbath dinner. I bought a half-priced honey cake. You still like honey cake, Gustav, yes?" I ask gently. He looks at me, his dark eyes unreadable, his dark curls falling onto his forehead, his right hand massaging the injured left one.

"Yes, Hannah, I still like honey cake. I look forward to the honey cake. Now I am going back upstairs to listen to music and try to compose. Long ago I vowed to write a viola concerto, and I am determined that I will write one. Please excuse me. If there is something you need help with that is too heavy or that you cannot reach, call me and I will help." He carries his dishes to the sink and goes upstairs. The radio clicks on.

On Friday morning I scrub, sweep, and dust. It does not take long. Our unassuming gray frame house is thin and small: kitchen, parlor, bathroom, two bedrooms. Upstairs, what was an attic is now one room with a small half-bathroom. It is Gustav's music room. Outside is a small yard with a large red maple tree, scraggly grass, and many weeds. A metal storage shed holds snow shovels, rakes, a watering can, garden tools, and three folding lawn chairs. I plant flowers each year. I like the cheerfulness of marigolds. The reparation money we receive, plus Gustav's disability payments, cover our rent and expenses and now Johanna's tuition, if we are careful. My job is to make sure we are careful. I know when and where the sales take place. Our clothes and furniture come from Goodwill, Salvation Army, and thrift shops. We can walk to almost everywhere we need to go, and a city bus stops nearby if we need to travel farther. Johanna takes the bus to the city university. Our landlord does any big repairs willingly because I never bother him about the small ones. In the winter I sprinkle the steps with salt. In the fall I rake the leaves. I replace burned-out light bulbs. I paint flaking window sills.

Johanna comes home from school in a good mood. "The professor said I am doing very well, Mama," she says. "He thinks I will have no trouble finding a teaching job."

"Very good," I say. "You will be a wonderful teacher. Wear the nice dress tonight." The nice dress is the one I found at the good thrift shop. Its melting watercolor flowers on high-quality cotton remind me of Mama's flower garden. We had so much sunshine and such beautiful roses and peonies. Johanna rolls her eyes but says nothing.

"Do you need help with the dinner?" she asks.

"No," I say. "The fruit is stewed. There's nothing to do but heat the soup and toast the bread when our guest comes. We will use the good plates and goblets, the nice tablecloth, and the cloth napkins." I suddenly realize that I do not know the young man's name. What kind of mother invites a young man to dinner to meet her daughter without knowing his name?

"I don't know his name!" I blurt out. "I didn't ask! He didn't say! I don't know his name!"

"Then we will all introduce ourselves at dinner, Mama," Johanna says gently. She takes my hand. "It's fine, Mama. It's fine. He will tell us his name."

I thought I would need to remind Gustav to put on his white shirt and come downstairs, but at six o'clock we three are sitting in the parlor, hands folded, in our good clothes, when we hear a knock at the door. I get up and open it, and there is the young man whose name I do not know, his hair wet with comb marks, holding out a small carton of raspberries.

"Come in, come inside," I say, taking the raspberries and beckoning him in. "Come inside and meet my daughter and my husband, Johanna and Gustav. I am Hannah. But I feel so foolish that I do not know your name!"

"My name is Joseph," the young man says.

"Joseph, thank you for the raspberries," I say. "Please, come inside and sit down." I guide him to the parlor, where Gustav and Johanna sit on the sofa, and point to a chair. Joseph sits down. I take the other chair.

"This is Joseph," I say. "Now I will go heat the soup and call everyone to dinner in a little while. Does anyone want ice water to drink?" I ask. No one does. "Then I will put the raspberries in the kitchen and call everyone to dinner soon. Johanna, if our guest is interested in seeing our family photographs on the table, please show them to him." From the kitchen, where I am heating soup and toasting slices of corn rye, I hear the murmur of voices but cannot make out the words.

"Good," I think. "At least they are talking. And if nothing else, I will eat fresh raspberries tonight." They are my favorite fruit, both fresh and in jam. Each summer my mother made raspberry jam, which she spread on my buttered roll at breakfast. My birthday cake had raspberry jam between the yellow layers and fresh raspberries on the lemon icing. Fresh raspberries are too dear to buy in this life, but how wonderful that tonight we will each have a few with our dessert. I put one in my mouth and let its tart sweetness dissolve on my tongue. Then I ladle hot soup into three bowls and arrange toast on three plates.

"Come to the table, please!" I call. "Dinner is served!" We eat in silence, except when Joseph says, "Everything is delicious." He eats as if he is starving. There is lentil soup with potato and onion and split pea soup with rice and carrot. There is toast and butter. There is challah. There is ice water in heavy goblets. Spoons and knives clink gently. The sounds make me think of music.

"Do you play a musical instrument?" I ask Joseph. Now Joseph is methodically dividing the potatoes in his soup into smaller pieces in an attempt to eat more slowly. I will serve seconds as soon as we finish our first bowls.

"I studied the trumpet at school," he says. "I liked it. I brought it home to practice, but my stepfather made me practice into a pillow so he didn't have to hear. He is a mailman and leaves for work very early, so by 3:00 pm, when he comes home, he wants to sleep. He doesn't want to hear music." Gustav winces but doesn't say anything. "Maybe someday I will take lessons. For now, I go to the community college and I work. I have one more course at the community college before I go to nursing school. I've been accepted with a scholarship pending completion of this last course. There are always jobs for nurses. Now, to pay my rent, I work part time as a teacher's aide at the elementary school near Salvation Salvage. I know that store from long ago. My father shopped there when I was a child."

"I am going to school to become an elementary school teacher," says Johanna. "Do you like being with the children?"

"I do," says Joseph. "I want to be a pediatric nurse." Just like that, the two of them begin to talk about schools and children and jobs. I lean back, take a breath, and look pointedly at Gustav, but he is looking down, tearing off bits of toast and putting them in his soup. "How could a man not want to listen to music?" he mutters.

"But do you like music, even if you don't play an instrument" he asks Joseph.

"Yes," says Joseph. "I like music. I have a small radio. In the night, if I can't sleep, I listen to music. If I can't think of words to explain something or understand something, I listen to music. But usually I am so tired from my class and my job that my problem is hearing my alarm clock in the morning, not falling asleep at night. But I like music."

"Good," says Gustav. "I too listen to music on the radio."

"Are you from this city? Do you have family here?" I ask. I want to turn the conversation away from music. Music is Gustav's dream. Maybe Joseph has a different dream. "And, if I may ask, how old are you?" Joseph turns from Gustav to me.

"I grew up here, yes," he says. "I am twenty-one. A family? It depends on what you mean by a family. I have a mother and a father who divorced when I was four. My mother remarried and had another child. My half-brother is five years younger than I am. Until I graduated from high school, I lived on the south side with my stepfather, my mother, and my brother during the week. I lived with my father on weekends and part of each summer, on the north side. My mother cares only that things look perfect from the outside, and to her, I am a mistake—the symbol of her failed first marriage. She says to people, "I have two boys and I love them both very much," but I am the frog and my brother is the prince. Last year, before I found this job, I lost my job and had no money to rent a room. I called my mother to ask if I could come home for a little while, just until I found a new job and could find a new room. She said no, it would look bad to the neighbors and her church friends if I came home." The words spill out of him. He looks down, twists his napkin between his hands, looks up. "So that's my mother," he says. "My stepfather supports her in everything she says and does. And my father? My father cares only for money, even though he has a secure job," he continues. "That is one reason my mother left him. My father told me every day that my stepfather stole my mother away, but that is not true. She left my father because he is so difficult. I know Salvation Salvage very well because he took me there as a child. I remember tugging on his hand, trying to pull him away from bothering the cashiers for additional discounts. He always wants something for nothing. He would charge me more than any landlord to stay with him. So, yes, I have a mother and father, and a stepfather too, but no, I do not have a family. Sometimes the cafeteria ladies give me twice as much macaroni and cheese for half the price because they are kind. I talk to them, and they are like a family. When I look back and wish things could have been different, I remind myself that I was the child, not the adult, and that I could not make things different. Now I am the adult, and I will change things. Someday I'll have a real family, like yours, where there's love and concern." He continues eating his soup, more quickly now. "And music, too," he adds, looking at Gustav. "No more blowing trumpets into a pillow. There will be trumpets ringing through the house. Double trumpet concertos. And lots of wonderful soup and honey cake and all the raspberries anyone could want." He falls silent.

"I will get everyone more soup now," I say gently. "And then we will have dessert, with the raspberries Joseph brought." I ladle more soup into our bowls.

Gustav talks about his favorite composers, and Joseph asks questions, and Johanna chimes in, and I listen to them and feel content. I will always miss my parents and the childhood I didn't have, but I still must do what needs to be done. I know what Joseph means.

After we finish our soup, I bring out the honey cake, the fruit, and the sour cream. I put a slice of cake on each dessert plate and top it with a little sour cream. Then I spoon some stewed fruit on top of the sour cream and place several raspberries on the top.

"Thank you for the beautiful raspberries," I say to Joseph. "They are my favorite fruit."

"You are welcome," he says. "There is a fancy grocery store on Kingshighway. I like to go inside and walk around. The fruit and vegetables there are like an art exhibit. That is where I bought the raspberries. I am sorry the carton is so small."

"They are enough," I say gently. "Thank you."

We eat our desserts and go into the parlor. It is late, and it is warm, and Gustav dozes off on the sofa. Joseph and Johanna talk quietly about school, and for a few moments I imagine a future for them. Then I get up.

"I'm going to finish up in the kitchen," I say. "You two talk as long as you like." In the darkening kitchen I wash the dishes and sweep the floor. Then I sit at the kitchen table and cut myself another slice of the honey cake. I love the sweetness of honey cake. I sit there, nibbling at my cake and watching the sky change from blue to indigo to midnight. Perhaps I doze off for a few minutes, in the summer heat, because when I open my eyes Joseph is standing before me.

"Johanna has fallen asleep on the sofa," he whispers, "and I need to head home. I have to be at work at 8 am. I want to thank you for inviting me to your Friday dinner. It was wonderful." He reaches out his hand to shake mine, and I hold onto his hand for a minute, trying to find the words to ask if he will visit us again. Did he like Johanna? Is he interested in seeing her again?

"Hannah, the nursing school is in Cleveland," Joseph says gently. "Next month I am moving there. It is a three-year program, and if I like Cleveland, I will find a job there after I graduate. Johanna is a very nice young lady, and you and Gustav are very kind. I think you would like me to be interested in Johanna, but I cannot be interested in another person now. Any person. Sometimes I don't think I can even take care of myself. But we all must take care of ourselves, isn't that right? If we are fortunate, we grow up with parents who care, parents who are there, people to help, and people who are kind. You and I are alike, I think. We were not able to be children, but we must still be adults. That is hard. I am not yet able to take care of someone else. Perhaps I never will be. Thank you for inviting me here tonight. It was very kind of you, and I will always remember this evening. Please find the time to take care of your dreams too, Hannah, and not just everyone else's dreams."

"You as well, Joseph," I say. "Please come back and visit us before you leave for nursing school in Cleveland."

"Thank you," he says, and turns to leave.

I go back to the living room and nudge Johanna to go upstairs to bed. "Morning comes soon enough," I say. Once she has climbed the steps slowly and I hear the door to her room close, I wake Gustav and say, "We are making some changes here starting tomorrow. I still want to be a librarian, and you will help me become one. I have been helping you. I need you to start helping me."

A few years later, Johanna will marry another teacher in our back yard, under the maple tree's red-gold canopy of autumn leaves. I will graduate from library school the following spring and find a job as a children's librarian. Gustav will finish his viola concerto, plus a song cycle for viola, voice, and piano. This city's symphony will decide to perform the concerto, and the Cleveland Symphony will decide to perform the song cycle. A surgeon in Cleveland will hear of the song cycle and will offer to repair Gustav's hand for free, so that Gustav can again play the viola professionally. While the surgeon operates on Gustav's hand, I will walk restlessly around the hospital campus, thinking of Joseph. I will go inside the School of Nursing, but no one can or will give me information about him. He did not visit us again before he moved to Cleveland, and he was not at Salvation Salvage on Thursdays. Perhaps he now works in Cleveland. Perhaps he graduated nursing school and left Cleveland for another city. It is true—there are jobs for nurses everywhere. Perhaps he never went to Cleveland for nursing school. Perhaps what he told us was not true. I don't know his last name or how to find him.

Several days after Joseph came for dinner, while I dust in the parlor, I notice one of the photographs is gone. It is not the big one in the fancy frame. It is not the one of my parents. It is not my wedding photograph or any of Johanna's school photographs. It is the small blurry photograph the landlord took on the day we moved into this house—a young Johanna between a young Gustav and myself, our arms around her and each other, sitting on the front steps as we smile and squint into the sun. I would have given the photograph to Joseph if he asked. I hope he has it still, wherever he has gone.

Seeing You

The phone rang early Monday morning. I didn't answer, and the answering machine clicked on. "I'm selling the house," announced Catherine. "If you want any of your father's books, come take whichever ones you want." After she hung up, I decided to drive down to New Jersey that morning, while Catherine was at work. It's not that I don't like her. I do like her. When I was a child, she was more of a typical mother to me than my own mother was. I just didn't want to hear her tell me again that I look exactly like my father, although he never needed glasses and I've worn them since I was seven.

My father wanted me to become an ophthalmologist, like he was, since I was always interested in eyes. "Why do I need glasses?" I asked him when I got my first pair. "Why don't you?" He explained to me how the shape and curve of the cornea and the lens of the eye affect vision. I was intrigued, and for a few months I examined his eyes with a penlight that had no batteries. I didn't want to deal with patients, though. I didn't want to tell an old man that he had glaucoma and would never regain his peripheral vision. I didn't want to tell an old woman that she had macular degeneration and would be blind in a few years. I didn't want to get beeped in the middle of the night to operate on eyes that were beyond repair. I would rather bring good news. I work for a small lens company, here in Connecticut, called ClariVision. I've been developing equations for a progressive lens that has more fluid intermediate, near, and distance components than other trifocals on the market. Instead of placing the add-on power on one or both sides of the lens, I'm trying to cut the power completely through the lens. Not everyone knows that in myopia, the eye is too powerful, not too weak, for what it sees. I want to create a lens that relaxes the eye and lets it see more clearly.

This morning I'd drive down to New Jersey and sort through my father's books. Julia, my girlfriend, would love to own them all, but she'd settle gracefully for however many I brought back for her. My father had hundreds of books—not just medical books, but novels and poetry and biographies. He bought whatever he wanted, whenever he wanted it. I'm not much of a reader, and neither is Catherine, but my father could spend hours in a bookstore. He'd stop at one bookstore or another almost every day. Sometimes Catherine called him and said in a lighthearted way, "That's enough! Buy the book now and come home!" Julia also read constantly, especially novels and short stories. She was always trying to get everyone to read more.

My mother isn't a reader either. A small woman with a sharp chin and eyebrows arched like a gull's wings, she and my father met, and married, in medical school. After they graduated, she wanted to return triumphant to the city of her childhood, where she grew up poor. Now she lives in a gated development of leafy cul-de-sacs ringed by golf courses. They got divorced when I was four. I remember the evening my father left. It was early April, and it had been raining steadily for days. My father knelt down and put his arms around me. His face was wet.

I said, "You have rain on your face!" I didn't realize that his face was wet with tears. I had never seen him cry, although I had seen my mother cry many times and heard my mother and father fighting. I leaned against my father, who that evening smelled like dill and wet earth. He told me that he wasn't going to live with my mother and me anymore but that he would see me very often. You see, my mother was having an affair. Other doctors and nurses knew this long before my father figured it out. I knew only that my mother was happy again. She stopped asking my father to pay attention to her. She sang in the shower and put on lipstick with delicate, careful strokes.

After my father found out, he told her he was leaving unless she stopped seeing her lover immediately. My mother didn't want my father to leave, but she didn't stop seeing the other man. My father left. The other doctor returned to his wife, and then, one evening when my father came to pick me up, my mother asked him to come back to her.

"It's over," she said to him.

"It certainly is," he agreed, and my mother went crazy. By day she went to the hospital in her white coat and stethoscope, acting calm and knowledgeable. At night she sobbed and screamed and pounded her fists against the wall. One morning she broke all our dishes. On her days off, she drove by the house my father rented and threw garbage on the front lawn. She called my father late at night. She'd lean against the refrigerator and howl into the phone. She promised him she would kill herself if he didn't come back. I lay in bed, listening to my mother scream and threaten, understanding long before she did that no matter how much she wanted my father to come back, he wouldn't. Somehow, my mother managed to finish her residency and pass her medical boards. She found a position as an anesthesiologist. I started kindergarten. Between what my father and mother earned as doctors, I never lacked for material things.

When I was six, my father married Catherine. Catherine once told me that when she saw my father walk into the realty office, she jumped up before anyone else and asked, "May I help you?" My father was a handsome man, but he was impatient with being handsome. He bought the first condominium Catherine showed him and asked her to have lunch with him. After they married I still lived with my mother, but I spent as much time as possible with my father and Catherine.

Catherine took me to buy clothes and school supplies. She came to my soccer games and school concerts. She baked me cakes. It was Catherine who asked me if I had any questions about anything or if anything was troubling me. She was the one who told me why my father left my mother. Catherine was good to me. I don't know why my father and she never had a child. Perhaps she couldn't. Perhaps he wouldn't. My mother had my father's child but not my father. Catherine had my father but not my father's child. My father had his work and his books—and Catherine and me, of course.

My mother continued to call my father in the evenings, although less often. Sometimes she'd make lists or idly rearrange the contents of the refrigerator while she wept into the phone. When I was in high school, my father and Catherine moved east, and I decided to apply only to colleges in the east. This did not sit well with my mother, who hoped I would stay in the Midwest. I chose

Tufts. I came home on holidays and called my mother every week. It was during one of those Sunday night calls when she said, "And has *she* cheated on him yet? Or doesn't Ms. Realtor need a husband who actually knows she exists?" I didn't call for a few months after that.

My father reminds me of a man who works at ClariVision who is obsessed with basketball. During the playoffs, nothing can distract him from watching the games.

"One time my wife stripped naked and stood in front of me during the game, and I just shooed her away," he told me proudly, reenacting how he had craned his gaze around her and motioned her away. He could have been describing my father, although what my father craned his head to see was medicine, not basketball. I believe my father loved me. I think he loved my mother. Why marry her otherwise? I've thought about the dates, and she wasn't pregnant when they got married. I think he loved Catherine, too, or at least he liked her enough to marry her. It's just that he considered love and passion to be leafy and suffocating, akin to living on a cul-de-sac. Love is not where my father wants to linger. For years after my father left my mother, she banged her head against the gate of his heart, hoping to be readmitted. Catherine understood my father in a way my mother never did. Catherine never seemed to mind that my father was always working or reading.

"Of course she minds," Julia said. "She just doesn't show it."

"Or maybe she's just glad to be married to someone smart, rich, and handsome," I answered.

"There's that," Julia said. "Plus she gets all the alone time she wants."

I drove to New Jersey through early-morning mist. After a while the sun shone through, but my thoughts wouldn't clear. Empty boxes jostled each other in the back seat, like quarreling children. Julia and I had argued the night before. She wanted to give up her apartment and move in with me because we spent almost every night at my apartment anyway, but I wouldn't let her. I knew it was sometimes hard for her to make ends meet on her salary, but I still didn't want her to give up her apartment. Besides, I paid for most of our expenses. We met at college. After we graduated, she followed me to Connecticut when I got the job at ClariVision. She found a library assistant job at the university while she tried to write the Great American Short Story Collection. "I read somewhere that novels are about worlds," she explained to me. "Short stories and poems are about feelings." Then, as now, I was about equations. She wanted to marry me. I didn't want to marry anyone. What was the point telling Julia she was the one for me and I for her? This way, when we broke up, there would be less turmoil.

When I pulled up outside the house where Catherine still lived, Catherine's car was gone. A yellow For Sale sign rose from the wet earth. There were no flowers now. Last fall Catherine had planted maroon, rust, and yellow chrysanthemums along the front walkway. In the spring she had planted pale pink and ivory tulips. All those colors looked good against the pale gray stucco. Today the house looked dreary. Inside the spotless kitchen I poured myself a glass of orange juice and headed for my father's study. Catherine had already taken down the curtains everywhere, and I looked across the lawn to the woods beyond. There were books everywhere—on the desk, in bookcases, and on the floor.

I filled one box with medical textbooks and journals for the library at ClariVision. Then I started placing books for Julia in the remaining boxes. I took fiction and poetry by authors with minimalist East Asian names; ornate Russian names; melodious South Asian names. I was surprised that I recognized as many authors' names as I did. Julia would be happy that I had listened to her book critiques.

After I filled three boxes, I turned to the nonfiction books. I pulled down a biography of an American doctor who traveled to underdeveloped countries to correct facial deformities. It seemed like a book my father would have, because he had always dreamed of opening his own eye clinic. But to do so, he needed a tremendous amount of startup money. When he and Catherine moved east, it was to accept a high-level job at a biotech company. If one of the drugs he was shepherding through development received FDA approval and the company went public, he'd make millions in stock options and bonuses. Then he'd leave and open his eye clinic, to run as he wanted. Catherine was holding her breath. She probably thought it meant she'd see more of him. I knew it meant she'd see less of him.

When I took the book off the shelf, an envelope fell out. It wasn't sealed. Several handwritten pages were folded around a small photograph of a middle-aged woman with glasses. I turned the photograph over. The back was blank. I turned the photograph over again and put my index finger on the woman's cheek. "Who *are* you?" I whispered as I traced her face from cheek to jaw. "What's your name?" I sat down at my father's desk to read the pages.

Happy birthday! This seems like a book you'd like. Perhaps you can read it on one of your many long flights to medical conventions.

It has been 30 years since you left me for Christine. Losing you so abruptly—and by telephone, no less--was terrible. It was an amputation. I sometimes think that your leaving me has been the pivotal moment of my life. I used to believe in pure happiness and straight lines. Once you left me, I became a different person—wary of happiness even when it beckoned. But what could I do except go on? I went on. I fell in love again, married, had a child, went back to school, bought a house...the usual things in the usual order. And then, one day, there you were online, answering a reporter's questions tersely, and looking frantic. I picked up the phone.

As I asked the receptionist to put me through to you, I imagined you and Christine, happily married after all these years. Why not? I'd still be married to my husband if he hadn't gotten sick and died. He was a good man, and we had a good marriage. I have a wonderful daughter whom I have always taught to break hearts instead of waiting to have her heart broken. "You never thought about me," I whispered to myself as I waited for the receptionist to connect us. Or maybe you did, in some vague way. "Oh yes, I think I remember her, but that was all so long ago." I was wrong. You had thought of me, and often. You had left Christine years ago. But you never called me. You married someone else instead. Why didn't you call me?

There's something I want to tell you now. That last year, when you were already in medical school, do you remember that I flew out to visit you several times? After the last visit you called me to tell me it was over between us. You had slept with Christine. You were in love with her, not me. I could only babble on about the set of plates my grandmother had promised us when we got married. My grandmother died a few years later. I don't know what happened to those dishes. I still wish I had them. I still wish I had you. At the very least, I wish you were mine for a longer time.

I should have realized during my last visit to you that things were very wrong between us, but I was too young to realize anything. I was also pregnant. When you called me to tell me it was over, I didn't yet know. Several weeks later, I found out. I had the abortion near the college. Of course it was too early to know if the baby was a boy or a girl, but I always imagined a boy, with your dark hair. He would be almost 30 now. He might have a family of his own. Sometimes, when I'm pinioned at the border of memory and sleep, I see him. He never speaks. I wave to him. He never waves back. When I call to him, he vanishes. Would you have married me if you had known? That's why I didn't tell you.

I never reconciled my loving you with your leaving me, as if those two facts were a mathematical equation. I still find it difficult to accept although I am single once again, I will travel the rest of my life without you in it.

It was wonderful to talk with you after so many years. One part of me would like to see you again. I imagine us having one of those intense, desperate, middle-aged affairs, all seedy motel rooms on the highway shot through with secrecy and tears. I've never done that, but I can imagine it. Another part of me thinks that you should leave your second wife and run away with me. Would you? I think not. But that second option is the only one I'm offering you—your third chance now, after 30 years, to be with me. Oh, it's easier for me, I know. I'm a widow. I don't have to break anyone's heart. But you had no problem, and no qualms, about breaking my heart 30 years ago. Perhaps you'll break someone else's heart this time, and mend mine. I hope you enjoy the book. Perhaps we'll talk again.

And there the letter ended, without a name. I looked at it until the black letters blurred. I put everything back in the envelope and put the envelope in my pocket. Did Catherine know? Had she found the letter? Had my father told her? Had anything happened? Had they met? Had she called my father again? Did he write to her? Did he call her? *Was* he planning to leave Catherine for her? I had always thought of my father as a victim and my mother as a villain. But here was another story. Julia says there are always many stories, of lovers and mothers and fathers and sons, of love and pain and grief and despair, of longing and lust and memory and youth and age. It was the kind of story she loved to read and I didn't.

I loaded the cartons into my car. As I backed carefully out of the long driveway, I took one last look at the house. I missed seeing the flowers. It would sell quickly. I would never see it again. I didn't care. This house wasn't my home.

I called Julia to tell her I was on my way. I didn't mention the letter or the photograph. As I drove back to Connecticut, I thought about the woman. What was her name? Did she know my father was dead? I decided not to tell Julia about any of this. I would find this woman on my own and give her back the book, the letter, and the photograph. Then I might tell Julia. Or maybe I wouldn't.

"These books are fabulous," Julia said. She was lying on my bed surrounded by dozens of books in various stages of invitation—open, shut, stacked, splayed, upside down. She was wearing gray sweatpants and one of my tee shirts. Her face was bright with the taste and touch of words. She blew me a kiss and turned back to the book she was reading.

I felt what I always feel when I look at Julia: desire mixed with longing mixed with sadness, as if we have already lived our lives together and are old friends, or as if we are characters in a book—the girl loves the one boy who won't marry her. I kissed Julia's cheek quickly, too quickly for her to turn and respond, and went into the living room. I felt like being alone and listening to music. What music did the woman in the photograph like? What was her name? Where did she live? Tomorrow, I'd call a few of my father's doctor friends and ask them if they knew of her. I lay down on the sofa as the room darkened. At some point I slept. When I awakened, I was still on the sofa and Julia had left for work. She had thrown a blanket over me and put my glasses on the coffee table. As always, I reached for my glasses before I sat up.

While I drank the remains of Julia's coffee I left messages for several of my father's friends. The pediatrician in Boston didn't know anything, and neither did the rheumatologist in Toledo, but the radiologist in Kansas City told me what I wanted to know. "She was your father's girlfriend when he was a senior and she was a junior," he said. "No one could believe he finally had a girlfriend. She was going to go to graduate school and write the great American novel while your father was in medical school." He wasn't curious about why I was trying to find her. "Sorry to hear about your father," he added quickly, before we hung up.

I did an Internet search; she worked at a library in New York City. I decided to take another day off from work and take the train down. If she were the right woman, I'd give her back everything and hope she wouldn't start weeping. Did she know my father was dead? If not, would she figure it out without my having to say anything? Maybe the alumni newspaper had published something. My father had been in a Japan for a medical convention. A train derailed as it flew into the station, killing several people on the platform. He was one of them. At Catherine's last birthday dinner, he had squinted at the menu and complained that it was getting harder to read the small print. He seemed distracted and fidgety, which was unlike him.

"You'll have to invent a pair of glasses just for me," he said.

"You? You can pick up a pair of reading glasses at any drugstore," I retorted. "You'll never need the incredibly sophisticated and advanced kind of lenses I develop." He laughed and closed the menu. Then he ordered the same thing he always ordered I don't know why he bothered looking at the menu. We came here every year for Catherine's birthday, although I don't think she really likes steak.

I called Julia from work and told her not to come over that evening. "I've got an early meeting in the city tomorrow," I lied. The next morning I was on the 7:10 to Grand Central, arriving a little after 9. It was a glorious morning—crisp and cool, with white shreds of clouds in a hard blue sky. I bought a pretzel and ate it as I walked. Leaves crunched under my feet and salt stuck to my fingers. The book was in my backpack. The letter and the photograph were in the envelope, inside the book. Every so often I'd reach behind me to make sure my backpack was still zipped and on my back. As I approached the library, I imagined my father and his girlfriend at college. He must have looked exactly like I look now, except for my glasses. I could see the two of them walking on campus, but I couldn't hear them. When I thought about my mother and father, what I remembered most was sounds: yelling and weeping and rain against the windows. When I thought of my father and Catherine, I remembered quiet and waiting: Catherine leaning over to check a pie or cake in the oven, or tilting her head in the dusk to hear if the garage door had finally opened.

Here was the library, and here were revolving glass doors to enter it. I had been frightened of revolving doors as a child until Catherine showed me how to maneuver them. This woman worked at a library. Perhaps my father got his love of books from her. Or maybe a love of books brought them together at college. I pushed the front door open, nodding good morning to the guard who sat on a stool near the entrance-and-exit turnstile. "I'm looking for her," I said, and showed him the name I had written down. "She's one of the reference librarians," the guard said. "Second floor, first office on the left."

I thanked him and began climbing the stairs. At the top I turned left, as directed, and almost immediately I saw her in her office, behind a desk piled high with books and papers. The office was small. The window faced an alley. The blinds were raised, and sunlight splashed in. The woman was pretty in a subdued way. Her reddish hair was mixed with gray.. Her glasses were similar to mine—titanium oval frames with a coppery sheen. If I wasn't mistaken, and I rarely am mistaken about glasses, they were progressive lenses that my company had developed a few years ago—not the ones I was currently working on, but an earlier generation. So she was highly myopic, like me.

She was talking softly on the phone and writing on a yellow pad. Although she gestured at me to come in, she didn't really see me. I stood in the doorway, watching her and looking around the office. Still without looking at me, the woman held up a finger and continued to speak and write. I suddenly felt uneasy. Could I really just put the book on her desk and leave without a word? When I imagined this moment, I thought I'd have her undivided attention from the second she saw me. Her mouth would open; I'd smile and put the book down; I'd turn around and leave. But the longer I stood there, the more awkward I felt.

I looked at the window and then back at the woman. With a soft flurry of final instructions, she said good-bye and put down the receiver. Her eyes met mine, and her face whitened. Her mouth opened.

"Please don't say I look exactly like my father," I thought. Neither of us spoke. I took the book out of my backpack and placed it near her hand. She put her hand on the book.

"I sent this to him," she said. "For a birthday present." She cleared her throat. "Then I read that he died. Obviously he received it. I don't know if he read it. The letter, I mean. Not the book. There was a letter inside the book. And a photograph. The letter was sealed. I'm sorry. I'm not making sense, am I? Are you a doctor, too?"

"No, I'm not a doctor," I said. "I make lenses. I think the company I work for made the lenses in the eyeglasses you're wearing. The letter was unsealed. He must have read it. I read it, too. It was in the book. It wasn't sealed."

My backpack felt heavy. My throat was dry. I took off my backpack and put it on the floor near her desk. Then the woman threw the book at the wall. It fell on the floor. We both looked at it and at each other. She seemed to be memorizing my face. After a few minutes she stood up and walked around the desk to stand next to me.

"Take off your glasses," she said.

"What?" I said. "I can't see a thing without them! I never take them off."

"I'm exactly the same way," she said. "But take them off anyway. Humor me." I shook my head in exasperation as she carefully took her own glasses off and put them in the middle of her desk.

"Please take off your glasses," she repeated.

"OK," I said. I suppose it could have been worse. She could have started crying, or fainted, or told me stories I didn't want to hear. I put my glasses next to hers. For a moment I wondered if she were going to kiss me, and how that would feel, and would I want to kiss her back, but she was staring straight ahead. She had stopped crying.

"Give me your hand," she said. I held out my hand, and she took it. Hers was cold. We stood side by side between the desk and the window, holding hands and looking toward the window. She began walking, and I— still holding her hand—followed her. We walked toward the window, which took about four steps because her office was so small. We looked out at the city.

"He had so much passion for medicine and his patients," she said. "I didn't really expect him to leave his second wife and run away with me. I just wanted him to say he wanted to! I called it a subjective road map. I just wanted him to want to. I just wanted him to say so. I wanted him to say that he loved me. That he *had* loved me. I thought I'd marry him. I thought we'd have children. He had three chances in life to choose me, and he didn't. It's like some tiresome old fairy tale that never turns out differently. I'm so tired of seeing it. I want to stop seeing it. I want to see something else." I nodded, even though I know she couldn't see me clearly. I couldn't see anything but blurry shapes and colors, even when I squinted. I was sure she couldn't see anything clearly, either. If anything, her glasses were thicker than mine. The expression "the blind leading the blind" crossed my mind. I sighed. I continued staring out the window as we held hands. Her hand had warmed itself on mine. How strange the city looked this way, like something the Impressionist painters would paint at the end of life, when they had given up trying to make sense of how things were and moved on to how things could or should be. The blurred colors and shapes *were* beautiful.

Who needed to see everything clearly at every moment? Without speaking, and still holding her hand, I tilted my face upward toward the sun. Even through the smeared window I felt its warmth. What a relief it was to shut my eyes.

"I did what you wanted me to do," I whispered to the woman next to me. "I took off my glasses." We were still holding hands. "Now do something for me. Shut your eyes. Please shut your eyes. Just for a moment, please shut your eyes."

The Piano Trio

The piano trio is on the radio right now. It's no longer played often, but sometimes, late at night or in the early hours of the morning, when all is as still as it ever is, a somber voice announces the trio and the names of its composers, and the lilting, questioning notes of the Allegro burst toward me. I've always felt that they beckon me to follow them. I'm in the half-dark at the kitchen table, staring into a glazed blue bowl filled with letters, lab results, notes to myself, scribbles of music, and advertisements. I never search for the piano trio, but when it finds me, I listen to it carefully, as if it can yet answer the questions I still have. As the number of classical music stations declines, I must look further afield to find one. This classical station is broadcast from a small college somewhere in New England. I can't remember the name. It doesn't matter. The announcer is young and talkative. I'm surprised to hear the piano trio from this college, at this hour, but here it is once more.

Half a century ago, when I was a conservatory student, I caused a short-lived and soon-forgotten stir by not attending the prestigious composition competition I had entered. I was eighteen, fresh from a small city in the Midwest, with huge ambitions to become a concert pianist and a composer. No one knew where my musical interests and abilities came from; my father was an accountant and my mother was a nurse. A neighbor who taught piano lessons from her home observed me lingering at her living room window to hear the music and suggested to my parents that I take lessons. My parents agreed and purchased a used upright piano. After a few years of lessons with my neighbor, I advanced to lessons at the university's music department. So it all began: my love affair with the piano and with classical music. I especially liked the music of Robert Schumann. I told my teachers that I wanted to write music like his music. I daresay it's more that I wanted to be Robert Schumann—so fascinated by and expressive about so many topics and emotions that he seemed to be several people, not just one—although I didn't have the words to articulate how I felt. I've come to realize that I've always been unable to express my feelings clearly, except in composing and playing music. But back then, I just knew that classical piano music, especially Schumann's music, brought me to life, and that every day I needed to play and compose and listen to music I loved.

After high school, I was accepted on full scholarship to a conservatory on the East Coast, with a dual major in piano and composition. My parents drove me the thousand miles east, they baffled but proud and I percolating with nerves and excitement. We found my solitary dormitory room. They gave me an envelope of money, reminded me to call and write frequently, said they loved me and were proud of me, and hugged and kissed me good-bye. My poor parents! They didn't understand me, but they loved me. I am older now than they were then. There I was: a thin, pale youth with wispy light-brown hair and delicate features, awkward around most people and especially around girls, with a tendency to stumble when walking, since I was perpetually composing music or working out keyboard fingering.

"I'm finally here!" I said out loud. I bowed to the window and the city outside. I unpacked my suitcases and, as the afternoon edged into evening, left my room to explore the campus. Tomorrow was the formal arrival day for students. This evening, I was apparently on my own. I hadn't seen anyone but the guard at the front desk, and I asked him where to find the practice rooms.

"Across the street," he said and pointed. "That building. Tonight you'll have your pick of practice rooms. Enjoy it! It won't ever be this easy again."

Small square carpeted rooms with baby grand pianos, music stands, and a few chairs lined both sides of the hallways on three floors. I went into one and sat down at the piano. Its tone was warmer and more receptive than my piano at home, and I happily began to play Schumann's short piece "Chopin," first softly and then loudly, as my delight at being here—at this piano, in this room, at this conservatory, in this city—erupted into the music. I was in the middle of the repeat when I heard someone open the door. Had I done something wrong? Was I disturbing someone? I had assumed the rooms were soundproof, but maybe they weren't. I turned around. Standing in the doorway was a young woman with deep-set brown eyes and dark-brown hair.

"I'm Chloe," she said, holding out her hand. "I'm a senior piano and composition student. I heard you playing. I love Schumann's music. Are you new?"

"Yes," I said, jumping up to shake her hand. "I'm a freshman. My name is Jeremy. I just arrived. I'm sorry if I disturbed you." At home I had few friends and no girlfriend, but being at the conservatory, surrounded by music and musicians past, present, and future, changed me in that moment into a confident youth who could jump up, smile, grasp a beautiful young woman's hand, and say, "Schumann is my favorite composer! I want to play everything he wrote and compose music like he did!"

"Then you need to meet my boyfriend," said Chloe. "He's also a senior, but with a triple concentration in cello, piano, and composition. His name is Reuben. He loves Schumann's music too. According to Reuben, Schumann said that "music is the language of the soul," and that's exactly how Reuben feels. I agree with him. Come and have dinner with us in the Student Union. We can talk more there." I felt a sudden loss, as if something I didn't know I wanted had appeared and disappeared, never to return. But I hadn't been expecting or even looking for a girlfriend, had I? I reminded myself that I had come to the conservatory to study music.

"Yes, thanks, I'd like that, " I said.

"OK then," she said. "Come on!"

The Student Union was almost empty. I followed Chloe to a table where a tall young man with curly auburn hair was writing in a composition notebook with his right hand and moving the fingers of his left hand on the neck of an imaginary cello.

"Reuben, this is Jeremy. I discovered him playing Schumann in a practice room. He's a freshman."

"Hello," Reuben said, looking up and dropping his pencil. His eyes were pale green, with a faraway look. "What's your major?"

"Piano and composition," I replied.

"Ah, like Chloe!" he said. "I started out with the cello and I never want to let it go, but I love the piano too. So I'm a triple major. "

We discussed our favorite composers and music over bowls of soups, plates of salad, self-serve soft ice cream, and a walk around the conservatory's small urban campus. My head filled with tall, narrow buildings, the honk of horns, clusters of yellow cabs, buses lumbering like arthritic dowagers from the curb to the middle of the street, the smoke of roasted nuts, the tomatoey tang of pizza.

"Someday I'll write a concerto to this city and my new friends," I thought. "I want to take my musical friendships as seriously as my music." When I at last arrived back in my room, I was exhausted and fell quickly into a deep sleep. We had made plans to meet at the registration tables in the morning.

I soon discovered that I was not a star—at least not yet, and most likely not ever. Every student at the conservatory was talented, and each had particular strengths and weaknesses. Only a very few, like Reuben, were stars. Chloe was not a star.

She never experienced stage fright and she played and performed well, but she struggled with composition assignments. Her compositions were easy on the ear, but they did not say much that was original. I was more comfortable composing than performing. I had gotten encouraging feedback on several short compositions, but I froze when playing them for anyone, even my instructors. Reuben was a very good cellist and a good-enough pianist with no performance difficulties, but composition was where he shone. The music that spilled out of him was a new language, overflowing with references to words, myths, numbers, fables, games, and secret codes and jokes. In it, he was two people: a fiery, impetuous adventurer and a serene, tranquil dreamer.

He carried notebooks everywhere and was forever scribbling, humming, and drumming his fingers on an imaginary keyboard or cello neck. He dedicated some of his pieces to Chloe, others to his musical and literary heroes, and one short, playful piece to me. That dedication meant a lot to me. At the time, I was composing my first sonata, and each day I found something that needed redoing. Still, my instructor said the sonata had good bones and to keep going. I kept going. I planned to dedicate it to Chloe and Reuben once I finished it, although there were many days when I feared I wouldn't finish it.

I sometimes envied Reuben. He had all that talent, and he had Chloe. I could see that she loved him. I thought he loved her, but that was harder for me to discern. His thoughts seemed to be elsewhere much of the time, even when they were together. He had so many interests. He belonged to a poetry group, and he was teaching himself Italian. Chloe was always touching him. She would put her hand on the side of his cheek or stroke his hair as she passed or leaned over to see what he was working on, but I don't remember seeing him express affection to her, at least not in public. What did I know, though? I was young, and I was in love with Chloe, and Reuben and she were older and a couple and thus mysterious to me. I know Chloe enjoyed my company a great deal and my devotion even more, since I was always willing to walk around the city with her, eating pizza or ice cream and talking about music, classes, other students, or whatever Chloe wanted to talk about. We studied together, and we ate together, even when Reuben was off somewhere. I was under her spell. Once, as we walked, she said to me, "I know you love me, Jeremy, and you are my dearest friend. I love you as a friend. But I am with Reuben."

Sometime that winter, a student piano trio competition was announced. Unlike other posted competitions, this one did not require three different instruments, three performers, and one composer. It merely required three instruments, three performers, and any number of composers. Reuben must have been in class, but when Chloe and I saw the posting, Chloe said to me, "We have to enter! Two pianos and one cello! You and I can compose the piano parts, and Reuben can compose the cello part. Composition by and for the piano trio! Look, the deadline isn't for a few months, late spring, and the performance is at the very end of the semester. We have time. Let's do it! It will be fun! Let's tell Reuben at dinner. I'm sure he'll agree."

Reuben did agree. He immediately started thinking about the cello solo and how we would weave the two pianos around it.

"Something plaintive," he said. "In a minor key. D minor. No, E minor. No, G minor. Let's do G minor. Chopin wrote a piano trio in G minor."

"Fine with me," said Chloe, and I agreed. Who was I to disagree?

"You two start on the piano parts, alone or together, or both," said Reuben. "I'll handle the cello. Once we all reach a good point, we'll work together. We'll find one of the practice rooms with two pianos. This will be a first: two pianos and a cello! I don't know any piano trio that has been scored for those three instruments, do you?" Chloe and I did not. But none of us could find a reason why we shouldn't compose the first one.

Most evenings, after classes, dinner, and homework, we worked on the piano trio.

"G minor and 4/4 time," Reuben reminded us. "Other than that, write what you know and love. We all like the same composers. We'll weave the three voices together once we have something to weave." What did I know and love? I loved music. I loved playing it and composing it. I loved Chloe. But I didn't love the way my notes or Chloe's notes sounded. Reuben's cello part was quickly wonderful: a murmured warning, a soaring yearning voice, plaintive whispers. The piano voices were the problem. Chloe's was shrill and mine was dour. They didn't work alone, together, or with the cello. Chloe and I began meeting in a practice room with two pianos, trying to combine our scores.

"Why is this so hard?" she asked me one evening. "We're students at the conservatory! We're talented! We've composed other pieces. Why is this so hard?" I didn't have an answer.

"Perhaps it isn't meant to be," I thought.

"I don't know," I said. "Let's try again. Switch back to the dominant key here"—I pointed to a measure—"and see if that helps." We tried that. It helped. We made the melodies less complicated. That helped. We kept working. Reuben, the cello part completed, concentrated on other compositions and performance assignments.

"Bring me the piano pieces next week or whenever you're finished," he told Chloe and me. "We still have time. I have too much other stuff going on this week."

One night that week I collapsed into sleep on the keyboard. I awakened to Chloe's hands touching my face. She unbuttoned my shirt and began to unbuckle my belt.

"Chloe, what are you doing?" I asked, as her hands guided mine to the buttons on her shirt. "You're with Reuben! I've never done this with anyone. I don't..."

"Shush," she said, cutting me off. "Don't say a word. Don't say a word about this now or ever. It's not happening. It never happened." She guided me down to the floor, under one of the pianos, and kissed me. I kissed her back, first cautiously and then hungrily, holding her tightly. After, I said, "Chloe, why? What does this mean?"

"I said don't talk about it," she said. "I mean it. Don't talk about it. You are my dearest friend. I'm still with Reuben. Nothing changes those two things." She got up and got dressed. I lay on the carpet, looking up at the underside of the piano. After Chloe left, I got up and got dressed and continued working on the piano trio.

"It's better," Reuben told us the following week, after listening to the piano parts. "We're almost there."

"Maybe it can't be done," I said. "Maybe that's the reason there aren't any piano trios for two pianos and a cello." He didn't answer. Chloe and I keep working. We finally finished the piano parts. Maybe the trio would make it to the finals because the cello part was lovely and the piano parts were finally good enough. I think all of us had given up hope of winning. I know I had. Sometimes I wondered why I was wasting time on the piano trio. I already had so much schoolwork and practicing to do. My teacher said I was making progress with my sonata. That was mine, mine alone. But I was so deep into the piano trio and so bewitched by Chloe that I just kept going. The next day, I played what I had written one last time and was happy enough with it. I gave my score to Reuben.

"I'm done," I said. "I can't work on it any more. Here's the score. Please don't lose it. It's my only copy."

That evening, I took a long walk by myself. I thought constantly about what had happened between Chloe and me, but the few times I tried to talk to her about it, she turned away. What had it meant to her? Why had she wanted to? "You are my dearest friend," she told me often. "I'm with Reuben." After my walk, when I returned to campus, I stopped by the practice rooms. Something about the nighttime sounds had inspired me, and I thought I'd work on my sonata. I was humming to myself as, head down, I pushed open a practice room door and saw and heard Chloe, Reuben, and a violin student whose name I didn't know playing the piano trio.

"Wait, what are you doing?" I cried out. "What's going on? Why is she playing my part?"

"Because it wasn't working with two pianos," said Chloe. "We'll give you composition credit for your part. Reuben and I decided we needed a traditional trio structure for the piece. We were going to tell you soon."

"But you're playing my piano part, Chloe!" I cried. "The violin is playing your part! My part is better than yours!"

"Your part is a better composition, Jeremy. I know that. But I'm a better performer than you are. You know that too." That was true.

"But it's my music!" I said. "Give me back my score!"

"And I'm performing your music exactly as it should be played," said Chloe.

"Chloe!" I said. "I thought we were friends!" I saw nothing in her eyes. Where was my best friend?

"Give me the score!" I yelled. Reuben and the violinist stood quietly. They said nothing. I saw nothing in Reuben's eyes either. The violinist looked down at the floor and sighed.

"I'm sorry," she said. She looked up at me. I saw compassion in her eyes. She looked down again. After a few minutes, the three of them began playing the trio. I watched them. And then I turned around and fled the practice room. I ran back to my dorm room and threw myself on the bed. I had thought Chloe and Reuben were my friends. For a brief interlude, I thought Chloe loved me and was going to choose me over Reuben. I was wrong. I thought we were the piano trio. I was wrong. I vowed to ignore them both forever and to be off campus when they performed the piano trio the following week. I berated myself for not making a copy of the score. Why hadn't I? Why had I trusted them? At that moment, I'm not sure what hurt more: losing my friends, losing the dream of Chloe, or losing my composition.

I did not attend the concert in which the four accepted entries—one of them the piano trio I had worked on—were played. As Chloe said I would be, I was noted in the program as the composer of the piano part she played. She was noted as the composer of the part the violinist played. That violinist went on to become a respectable performer in various chamber groups. I have that conservatory program still, buried somewhere under letters and other papers. The piano trio in G minor placed second. First prize went to a cheerful trio in D major for violin, viola, and French horn. Our piece, for I still thought of it as ours, was more haunted, more mournful, than the winning composition. I know Chloe was delighted to have placed second, and I know Reuben was crushed. All his life he had been first, and this was the first time he wasn't. My absence was commented on when I returned to campus, but I merely smiled when asked why I hadn't attended.

"Family emergency, but it's all fine now," I said.

I avoided Chloe and Reuben for the remaining weeks of the semester, and when my parents came to drive me home for the summer, I told them I planned to transfer to a conservatory in the midwest, closer to home, and that's what I did. After graduation I was asked to stay on as a faculty member, an offer I accepted with delight and gratitude. I taught, and I composed, for many good years, and I retired only a few years ago. Even now, some of my piano compositions are recorded, played, and taught. Although I had several serious, long-term relationships with women, I remained single. I was never in love again, and conversation, let alone emotional intimacy, was always hard for me. I heard that Chloe and Reuben married right after our May graduation and that their only child, a daughter, was born the following winter. They accepted faculty positions at a conservatory in New England. I also heard that Reuben died in an automobile accident when he was still quite young, and that Chloe and their daughter stayed on at the conservatory. The daughter grew up, married, and had her own daughter, according to what another musician told me a few years ago. I never tried to contact Chloe. She never contacted me. I'm still alive, so it is certainly possible that she is alive as well. She is only two or three years older than I am. I suspect we both would merit an obituary, and I have not come across hers. I remember reading Reuben's obituary and feeling nothing.

The piano trio is almost over. I lean forward as the last notes hover and then fade away. There is silence. Then the announcer's young voice continues. "This trio was originally written for two pianos and one cello by three students, but during its composition, one of the piano parts was transposed to violin. Why? Probably because no one has ever written a trio for two pianos and a cello. This piece won second prize in a student competition, and it has had a respectable life in chamber music circles, especially when quasi-Romantic pieces reminiscent of Schumann and Brahms are the rage. I still love it, maybe more so because my grandmother and grandfather were two of the three composers. I never met the third composer. My grandfather died when I was young, but my grandmother said the other composer was her dearest friend who had unknowingly given her the greatest gift of her life. I'm not sure what she meant, and she never would tell me. Her daughter, my mother, said she never knew either. My grandmother died a few years ago, and so her secrets about the piano trio died with her. In any event, I hope you enjoyed this wonderful music. Thank you for listening to it on this classical station."

I sit, my head in my hands, as morning approaches. Now I have new questions. I think Chloe used me to get pregnant. I know she liked me, and perhaps she even loved me, but she loved Reuben more. Did I love her? Yes. Was Reuben a star? Yes, he was. Even now his compositions ricochet across the musical universe. He is gone, but his music is as strong or stronger than ever. How did I miss Chloe's obituary? Here's another question: Am I this young woman's grandfather, as now seems likely? Did Chloe know that Reuben couldn't have children? Is that why she seduced me? I will think about these new questions while I sit here, waiting for morning. There's still time. There is always time, until there isn't. After I eat some toast with coffee, I will write a letter to this young announcer and tell her that I am her grandmother's dearest friend and fellow composer. I'll see if she responds. If she does, and if she is interested in hearing more, I'll write again. If she doesn't respond, "dearest friend and fellow composer" is not a bad epitaph. I hope she will write back and we'll start a conversation— her voice, then mine, then hers, then mine—melody and dissonance, harmony and grief, solo and intertwined, something original going somewhere new.

Rondo

In the middle of my thirteenth year I gave up playing the cello. It was November, and my parents had gone to Europe on a long-awaited vacation, leaving my younger brother and me in the care of our aunt. My parents may have told us that they would be away for several months, but I don't remember them telling us anything. One day my aunt was there and my parents were gone.

What I remember is sitting on the sofa with my aunt each morning, while I ate toast and she asked me what to do about my brother. The sofa had recently been reupholstered in dark green velour. I liked to stroke my palms against it and pretend I was lost in a forest. "Your brother's not eating much," my aunt said. "And I don't think he's taking baths or washing his face and hands."

I liked my aunt, who was soft to hug and sat as if she had been placed in a buttered bowl to rise. I told her not to worry about Daniel. "He's weird even when Mom and Dad are home," I said. This information creased her forehead, but she patted my arm and said, "Go to school." For once I didn't dawdle, or push all the buttons in the elevator on my way down, or walk down eleven flights of stairs. I hurried, because yesterday I quit the orchestra. Today was my first day as third clarinet in the band.

The orchestra met in the school's basement. Overactive steam pipes warred with the gasps and shrieks of string instruments. Mr. Wallinger was putting his violin into its case lined with velvet as bright as a sapphire. I told him I was quitting. His expression changed from tender concern to confused irritation.

"You are giving up first cello to be third clarinet? You want to play the dum-dum-dum while someone else plays the melody?" His hands mocked me. Then he shrugged and closed his violin case. He burst out:

"You are doing so well! You are taking private cello lessons!" Again he was silent. It did not occur to me to answer him. I stood mute, waiting for a sign that I was free to go. He shrugged again, and then he picked up his violin case and began walking toward the door. As he reached up to turn off the lights I slipped past him and ran up the stairs if I were being pursued.

I didn't stop running until I had burst into auditorium, where Mr. Hayford stood talking to several members of the band. Like the basement, the auditorium had no windows, but I felt as if I had left darkness behind and entered the blaze of day.

"You promised me I could join the band," I said to Mr. Hayford. "I need a clarinet."

"Someone get Beth a clarinet from the storage room. Give her a few reeds, and show her what to do." A boy ran off. His name was Willy Chen. We sat next to each other in science class. I waited for Mr. Hayford to ask me why I had left the orchestra to join the band. My mind was racing to phrase a single simple reason.

"Actually someday I want to play the piano," I blurted, although Mr. Hayford hadn't said anything to me and was polishing his glasses on his shirt.

Willy came back with a clarinet, a few reeds, and a book of exercises.

"Beth, I'd like you to learn the first two exercises by the end of the week," said Mr. Hayford. "Ask Willy for help if you need help. Class dismissed."

What I had blurted out was true: I wanted to play the piano. Our secondhand upright piano was delivered to the apartment when I was seven. It cost $200 and was the color of chocolate milk. It was delivered later than expected, so that my mother, tired of my ceaseless questions, banished me to the playground after lunch. When I returned at dusk, tired, thirsty, and dirty but no less excited, the piano was there. My mother sat on the wooden bench, playing delicate, flickering notes. Later I would circle the number of that magical Chopin nocturne and claim it as my own. Daily I marveled at the piano's cool keys and intricate carving. Each day I begged her to play the piano for me. Usually she would.

Surely my desire to play the piano was palpable since that day. At age ten, however, I was taking cello lessons. "Such a lovely mournful tone," my mother would say approvingly whenever she heard Pablo Casals on WQXR. Then I would be lulled into believing that I wanted to play the cello and that my mother and I were partners in this endeavor. The lessons continued. I progressed against my will -- too quickly for me and too slowly for my teacher, an elderly woman who once offered me a chocolate-covered grasshopper as a snack.

"Wait!" I wanted to say to someone. "The cello is too big for me."

Yet it was now a part of me, and I had to carry it to lessons and to school. It caught on rugs and hardwood floors. On the subway I bumped into poles and people.

My friends teased me. Strangers smiled or laughed or sometimes jeered.

The cello was large and curved and visible. I wanted to remain small and straight and invisible as I ran unencumbered through my city. I had mastered finding the notes. I had learned to read the markings for the bow. I could, according to my teacher, produce music. She decided that soon I would learn vibrato, that controlled movement of the left hand to create a note that is fuller, richer, and more emotional than a note played dead on. Faced with this ultimatum, which I knew would be followed by more difficult pieces, duets, and solo recitals, I waited until my parents were gone and my aunt was ensconced on our sofa. Then I cancelled my cello lessons and asked Willy Chen to help me learn the clarinet.

Willy was the first boy I wanted to kiss. He played the trumpet, and the curve of his upper lip was a small scrolled pitcher. Over the past year we had spoken little; we communicated by pen fight. The slashes of blue were hard to scrub off, so I left them on my arms to fade.

Without any discussion, Willy and I began to leave band practice together. At first we'd walk to the music store and buy reeds for my clarinet. Because my parents were away I felt no need to go home, telling myself that I was all alone and doomed to shiver in a thin coat and no gloves while everyone else ate hot food in bright kitchens. In fact my aunt was solicitous, willing to cook me whatever I wanted, and interested in hearing about my day, but it suited me to pretend that Willy and I were unloved rebels as we walked down Houston Street. I kept my hand in his jacket pocket for warmth.

Sometimes we'd go to Willy's house to tease Warren, his younger brother, who sat in front of the living room window wearing a white scarf and pretending to be a pilot. Then we'd sit on the floor of Willy's room and play Scrabble or practice our instruments. One day we began going to Rosie's Hero Shop, and that routine pleased us so much that, until our last day together, we never wavered from it. Then Willy would walk me home, disappearing silently as I opened the door.

"Beth?" my aunt would call from the living room, where she sat reading a book or listening to the radio. "Beth? Is that you?"

"Yes," I would say on my way to my room, where I would practice my clarinet until I went to sleep. My cat watched with cautious interest. Daniel remained barricaded in his room. Sometimes my aunt drifted around the apartment, dusting and straightening and humming to herself, no doubt counting the days until she could go home.

"Shall I take you anywhere?" she would ask every weekend. "Is there something special you want to do?" I shook my head no. I wanted to practice the clarinet and be with Willy.

I was second clarinet by the time my parents came home. My aunt went home, and my brother emerged from his room. Willy was required to come into the apartment when he brought me home. He and I still bought reeds and walked for miles after band practice. Winter passed without my being aware of anything except the square slabs of sidewalk on Houston Street, the linty flannel inside Willy's jacket pockets, and the sour taste of new reeds against my tongue.

The day Willy and I took the ferry to Staten Island was the last day we ever spoke. It was late April, and I had just turned thirteen. We met at the bus stop in front of the movie theater. Willy carried cartons of fried rice for our picnic. "You're so pretty," he said suddenly, and then blushed tomato red. I imagined us sitting in the grass on Staten Island, like those mysterious older couples whom I watched and envied.

On the ferry we stayed outside and watched the water breaking against the boat. It was cold and windy. Willy held my jacket sleeve, just above my wrist. Without speaking he led me off the ferry, through the terminal, and onto a bus. As we rode, we looked out the windows for a park. Wasn't Staten Island supposed to be the country? The bus went down one wide avenue after another, all spattered with shoppers and stores and cars. The rice turned cold and began to leak through the cardboard.

"Maybe this wasn't a good idea," Willy finally said. "Maybe we should just go back and eat in the terminal."

I saw that I could travel a parallel route all my life and never reach my destination. Willy and I would never have our picnic. I had given up the cello, but I was no closer to playing the piano. We were just thirteen, after all. Willy's hair was ruffled from the wind. He was chewing on his lip. He was young and baffled by my silence. I wanted to say, "Let's go back to the terminal and eat lunch inside before we head back," but I couldn't speak. I couldn't look at him. At the terminal he threw the cartons of rice toward a garbage can. One carton missed and splattered on the floor. We sat in silence, first on a damp green bench and then on the ferry ride home.

At graduation in June I was first clarinet. My mother and Mrs. Chen exchanged greetings, but Willy and I ignored each other. We hadn't spoken since April. We would attend different high schools in September. I sat on the stage in my white dress, my curly hair pulled back hard against the June sun, and listened to the melody undulate from my clarinet. Perhaps Mr. Hayford heard it too, because he looked right at me and said, "Very good!" But maybe he was talking to us all. After graduation I returned the clarinet and music to the storage room. I kept all the reeds, but over the summer some dried out, and my cat batted some under the furniture.

"Stop chewing on that thing!" my father yelled one evening, and I threw the last reed away. It was chipped and splintered to half its former size. If I saw one now, I would marvel that I once knew how to use something so specialized and so delicate.

The year before I went away to college I started taking piano lessons, but there was no real magic associated with them or the music, not in the way there had been on the day the piano was delivered. At college I couldn't practice often enough, and I forgot most of what I had learned. In my junior year my aunt died. In my senior year Rosie was murdered, stabbed to death on the ferry that Willy and I had taken to Staten Island.

Last week my mother called to ask me if I wanted the cello. She was cleaning out closets and asked if I wanted various papers and books. Then she mentioned the cello.

"It was your aunt's cello," she said. "Did you know?"

I hadn't known that. Or had I? I suddenly saw the cello, hunched over in its mildewed cotton case, trapped in the hall closet between the vacuum and the broom. When had it shrunk? I wanted to play the piano so desperately to free myself from the cello so frantically. Where have those desires gone? I have a piano now. It sits in the dining room, piled high with newspapers and library books. I pass it many times daily yet play it rarely.

"You should take lessons again," my husband urges. Now it is the cello that tugs at me. It seems smaller now, and it would be easier to handle. Knowing where it is and that its fate is in my hands reminds me once again that I have lost them all: my aunt, dead; Willy, somewhere unknown; Rosie, murdered; and me, the girl who ran so quickly through her city. I never got to kiss Willy. I never thanked my aunt for taking care of me for the month my parents were away.

My mother is still talking.

"It's not in great shape," she says. "I took it in to the music store to see if it can be repaired."

"That's good," I say, without really listening. I think about the cello. It is across the river, holding out its arms to me. I will drive into the city that is no longer my city and bring it here. I will have it repaired. I will take cello lessons again. I will take piano lessons and cello lessons. Yes. No. I can. I can't. I will leave the cello in the closet and let it continue uninterrupted on its solitary journey of defeat and decay. Some things cannot be made sense of or even examined too closely, let alone repaired or replaced. No. I need to go get the cello right now. I will leave for the city as soon as I hang up the phone.

"Let me know what I should do about the cello," my mother says, interrupting my reverie. "I can get it repaired if you want. Or you can take it and decide what to do with it later. The man at the music store told me there's some point of no return with all instruments, but he doesn't think we've reached it yet with the cello. Listen, I have to go now, and I'm sure you have things to do, too. I'll call you over the weekend, OK?"

"Yes, OK," I finally say, still holding the receiver to my ear, long after my mother has hung up and is gone.

Waiting

I park in front of Julie's house. It's Saturday; she's invited me to go swimming at the community pool. Her friend Becky answers the door. Becky is wearing a gauzy black shirt over a bathing suit; the skin under her eyes is smudged black as her shirt. Holding the door open for me, she says, "Thank you for your note. I'm glad to meet you, finally."

Becky is sleeping on Julie's sofa until she can find her own apartment. Today is Saturday; on Monday Becky came home to the apartment she shared with Sam, her fiancé, with a bag of groceries balanced on each hip. Before she could put them down he told her that he was in love with someone else. He offered to let her keep the apartment, but Becky turned around and went to Julie's apartment without letting go of the groceries. At Julie's, she wrapped chicken parts in plastic and put the carton of milk in the refrigerator before she started crying.

Julie told me that Becky has been staying up very late, playing music too loud and keeping busy in the kitchen. On Wednesday night, shortly before midnight, Julie found Becky making green beans vinaigrette. She explained to Julie that the proportions of sugar and lemon juice had to be exactly equal. She asked Julie to wait up with her until the beans were chilled, to taste them. Julie convinced Becky to go to bed.

This image upset me. I could not stop seeing a woman bent over in an ill-lit kitchen, her window the only rectangle of light in a dark building. The image superimposed itself on my pillow at night and in the bottom of my coffee cup at dawn. I could not forget it, and so I wrote Becky a short note, telling her how sorry I was that Sam had left her.

Standing at Julie's door, I say again, "I'm so sorry," and put out my hand, as if to balance some of her tiredness and pain. Julie comes down the hall, tying the neck of her bathing suit.

"Hey," she says. "Gil wants to come with us. Mind if we wait for him?"

"Fine," I sigh. Gil will be late, and I want to get to the pool. It's summer, it's hot, and my joints feel funny, as if they're glued together incorrectly. They don't hurt, but they feel wrong. Gil is always late. Gil is the reason that Danny, Julie's husband, moved out last month. Danny wants Julie to stop sleeping with Gil, and then he will move back. He writes Julie long, impassioned letters in which he promises to forgive or forget that Julie, despite being married to Danny, slept with Gil several times and plans to continue doing so. Julie has not answered Danny, and she is spending more and more time with Gil. She and I argue about this. I tell her, "It's not fair to keep Danny hanging. Tell him yes you'll stop sleeping with Gil or no you won't, so he can get on with his life either way and you can get on with yours. What's the problem?"

I go into the living room and sit down on the sofa. Becky's blanket is folded on the arm. When Danny moved out, he took the chairs from the living room and left the sofa. In the dining room, the table, chairs, and china cabinet are gone; wineglasses and ceramic casserole dishes stand guard in dusty corners. The smaller room, which used to be Danny's study, contains nothing but sunlight. Only the larger bedroom retains any semblance of comfort and normalcy, like before.

Julie sits down next to me, and Becky sits down at the other end of the sofa. She picks up the newspaper and begins looking at apartment rentals. I want to ask Julie if we can leave Gil a note on the front door and just go, but I know she won't leave without him. The words remain in my throat, unleavened. I get up and look out the window at the bright, cloudless day. Without turning around, I ask Julie what time Gil said he'd be here. "Around 1:00," she says. It's almost 2:00. I keep looking out the window. A man across the street trims a hedge. A child bounces a pink rubber ball on the sidewalk. Then I see Danny's old green car nose into a space across the street. I tell Julie, and she jumps up, cursing. "Danny said if he ever saw Gil here, he'd beat him to a pulp." She makes a face, as if Danny is being irrational.

When Danny knocks, Becky answers the door. The two couples—Julie and Danny, Becky and Sam—often did things together. They would cook dinners for each other and take weekend trips. Danny looks pleased to see Becky. "Hey, babe," he says. He hugs her and kisses her cheek. He says hello to me. We do not know each other as well. Then he asks Julie if she can give him some money. While Danny is in limbo, he refuses to open his own checking account. He is wearing tennis whites, and his fair skin is sunburned. "How is your game?" I ask, to fill up the silence. "I hurt my back, so not that great," Danny replies. "But I'm still playing." That's like Danny; once I invited Julie and him to my apartment for dinner. When they arrived, he looked pale and said he hadn't slept well.

"We could have canceled," I said.

"I thought you must have spent a long time cooking," he said. "I didn't want to disappoint you by not coming."

Julie gives Danny some tightly folded bills. He puts the rectangle of green into his pocket and then puts out his hand, as if to encircle her shoulder or her waist, but his hand stops short, traces the air, and returns to his pocket. Instead, he asks if he can have some ice cream. "It's so hot," he says. Julie hesitates and then agrees. Danny goes into the kitchen, and Becky follows him. From the sofa I can see him eating directly from the half-gallon container of butter pecan, gesticulating with an ornate silver spoon. Beads of condensation shimmer softly to the floor. Becky is talking softly and shaking her head. Danny smiles and replies, and Becky taps him on the arm. For a minute I imagine that Julie will choose Gil and then Becky and Danny can become a couple.

I look away from them and out the window. It's still sunny, but it's after 2:30, and the buildings are starting to cast slanted shadows on the street. Julie sees me looking outside and says, "Oh, fine, let's just go. I'll leave Gil a note." She says this as a present for me. We haven't been spending as much time together as we used to. For a few minutes the tension between us subsides, and we smile ruefully at each other. Then Julie calls to Danny and Becky to hurry up. Becky offers to drive. Julie writes a note for Gil and tapes it to the front door, where it makes one half-hearted attempt to flutter and then collapses in the mid-July humidity. I see Danny reading it as we file out one by one and start down the narrow stairs. I wonder if he knows—but of course he must know or, worse, imagine—that Gil spends nights here with Julie; that in the morning, while Gil lies wrapped in sunlight, Julie cooks him eggs and pancakes and brews strong coffee; that they shower together in the small, tiled bathroom; that Gil leaves for work complacent, loved, and fed. These images remind me of what Julie has done. I do not want to meet Danny's eyes, and I am glad to be the first one down the stairs.

I hear the three of them not far behind me as I reach the cramped vestibule and put my hand on the front doorknob. There is Gil, on the other side of the glass. He is blond and gray-eyed in a faded blue tee shirt, camera strap slung over his shoulder. "Danny's on his way down," I say. "Go back to your car." Gil looks at me, puzzled, not understanding. "Go!" I repeat, motioning him away. Then he understands and turns around. I push open the door and catch up with him, as if we are any two people walking. I don't talk, because I can see he is nervous. I fall back as Gil crosses the street to his car, just as Becky appears at my side saying, "What bad timing!"

Behind us, Danny is screaming at Julie, who is holding him back. "Do you want me to go out of my head?" He pulls free and begins running toward Gil, who is now standing at his car. Danny's face is red. Julie is crying. Becky and I encircle her and gently push her into Becky's car. Everything is bright and slow, as if underwater. Becky has trouble getting the car in gear. My eyes linger on the bright green leaves overhead, on the thin scarlet strap of Julie's bathing suit crossing her shoulder, and on Becky's worried face. As Becky's car lurches past Gil and Danny, I turn around and see Danny standing too close to Gil. Julie is still crying. Between sobs, she says, "Gil doesn't know how to fight! Danny will hurt him!" I want to say something, but I don't know what to say. Instead, I hug Julie clumsily.

We arrive at the pool. Julie says, "You two go in and find chairs. I want to call Gil and make sure he's OK." She has stopped crying, but her eyes are puffy. At poolside Becky and I spread out our towels on two chairs. The hard-blue sky is now tinged with gray. Only a few people are swimming. At the far end, a boy lifts a girl and drops her back into the water. She squeals—half in fear and half in delight.

Julie comes back to Becky and me and says, "I have to leave now. Gil is picking me up. He and I need to talk. He says he and Danny almost came to blows." Becky does not look up. Her eyes are closed. I silently repeat the words "came to blows" while I look up at Julie. They sound comic and melodramatic, like an old silent movie. "But, please, you two stay and try to have fun," Julie says as she walks away.

Becky and I stay. I don't feel like swimming anymore, and I guess Becky doesn't either, because she continues looking at apartment rentals in the newspaper. I stare at the pool and the trees. Suddenly Becky says, "I can't believe the things I've heard this year—the lies, the affairs, the double lives people are leading." She pauses, as if to give me an example, and then shrugs and bends back to her newspaper. She reads in silence, occasionally circling something, as the sky darkens and the wind picks up. "Would you mind if we go?" she asks. "I think it's going to rain." I tell her I don't mind. We fold our towels and put on our shoes. I ask her if she wants to get a cup of coffee somewhere, but she says she wants to go look at some apartments. "I can't stay at Julie's too much longer," she explains. "Being there is awkward, and that sofa is uncomfortable for sleeping. I need to find my own place and get on with my own life."

Becky drives me back to my car, which is parked around the corner from Julie's building. As I get out, I say, "Take care." I am conscious of how inadequate those words sound. I touch Becky's arm quickly, right above the elbow, and she leans over and kisses me on the cheek. "Thank you," she says. "That's kind of you. I'll be OK. Not now, not soon, but someday. I know I will. You take care, too." "Sure," I say. I smile at her and shut the car door. We both wave, and then she drives off.

I sit on the front steps of a building near my parked car as the sky continues to darken. I wish Becky had wanted to go out for coffee. Right now I'd like to be part of the normalcy and clatter of bright lights and silverware. I want to listen to people talking loudly and rapidly about their ordinary days and predictable lives. I used to be one of those people traveling through ordinary days, planning a delicious life with the beautiful boy I loved. Then last summer he left me for someone else, in one of those random thoughtless ways that people leave each other. "I met someone else," he told me. "I love her, not you," he said. "It's nothing against you," he added. "You're great. And we can always be friends, if you want." That's not what I wanted.

Julie is probably at the diner now with Gil, drinking coffee and eating pie. "He likes blueberry pie as much as I do," she once told me. "Danny hates blueberry pie. He hates all fruit pies." She will comfort Gil over coffee and pie, and maybe they'll end up sharing a burger or some macaroni and cheese for dinner too, although after dessert instead of before. Comfort food. After they finish eating, they'll laugh about how good the food tasted in reverse order and drive back to Julie's apartment.

I continue sitting on the steps, although the concrete is not at all comfortable and I feel drops of rain on my head. Julie has moved effortlessly from one love to another, and she may yet change her mind or never have to choose between Danny and Gil. Becky seems determined to make a new life, and I think she'll succeed. But what happens when a person can't move forward? I know I need to get back to my own life and stop living on the margins of other people's stories. I know that.

I sit a little longer, listening as the wind howls and the sky collapses into gauzy, smudged black. No one else is outside. This city has a reputation for brief, dangerous summer thunderstorms and tornadoes. When the storms arrive, everyone goes inside. Everyone except me is somewhere else. I stand up slowly and pull out my car keys. My joints still feel funny. Maybe I should make an appointment to see a doctor. As I open the car door and ease myself inside, the sky opens up and the rain pours down. I slam the door shut. I put my head on the steering wheel and shut my eyes. I wish Becky had told me about the double lives people are leading. Maybe it would help me figure out how to live one life: my own.

Apartment for Rent

I lived on one side of the city and worked on the other. Although I could easily have taken the highways the locals call the Innerloop and the Outerloop between my apartment and the office, I chose to drive the boulevards instead. They were lined with massive sycamores that provided breeze and shade, and I never knew what store or sight I might encounter. Driving the boulevards, I found a factory that made painters' pants, a butcher who made five kinds of sausage, a pancake and waffle restaurant that was completely underground, and a confectioner who made different types of licorice.

When I told co-workers about my discoveries, they were amused.

"You know more about this city than the people who grew up here," one said.

One day, on my way home, I saw a sign for a cafeteria and decided to stop for dinner. I grew up in a city with many cafeterias, and I hoped that this cafeteria might be like my childhood memories. I turned left off the boulevard, turned left again, and drove down a gently sloping street to a small parking lot outside a well-lit restaurant. I hadn't known this little neighborhood was here, although for a minute or two it seemed familiar to me. The houses were small duplexes or cottages, and all were surrounded by masses of flowers.

"Must be good soil here," I thought.

Although the boulevard was only a few blocks away, I could barely hear traffic noise. I went in the cafeteria and asked the server for macaroni and cheese and a bowl of vegetable soup. I carried my tray to a table. The food was good, but it was the sense of peace I felt that made me smile and let out a sigh of contentment.

"Are you local?" asked the woman who dished up my food.

"Well, I live and work in the city, but I'm not originally from here," I said. "And my lease is up soon, so I'm not sure if I'll stay here or move back to where I'm from."

"There's an apartment for rent in that white duplex right across the street, if you're interested. If you want to leave a $50 deposit with me and your phone number, I'll give it to the landlord, and he'll call you."

"I don't have my checkbook with me," I said, which was true, but I also wanted to think about it a little more. "Can I just leave you my phone number, and he can call me tomorrow? I can come down here after work and see the apartment. I pass this way all the time."

"Yes, leave your number with me," she said.

I wrote my home and work phone numbers down on the back of the receipt and handed it to her, and she folded it and put it in her apron pocket.

"This place is wonderful," I said. "I really enjoyed it. I hope to see you again."

I paid my bill, and she thanked me.

"Good-bye now," she said.

When I got home, I put my checkbook in my handbag, in case the landlord called while I was at work the next day. He didn't call, though, and I decided to stop by the cafeteria on my way home and ask to see the apartment. There wasn't a sign where I thought I remembered it, and the street I drove down after leaving the boulevard didn't lead me anywhere except to cul-de-sacs of ranch houses with children playing in the yards and parents coming home from work.

"Where's the cafeteria near here?" I called to one man.

"No cafeteria near here," he called back. "The closest restaurants are on the boulevard, but there's no cafeteria there either."

I drove around for an hour or more looking for the cafeteria, but I never came across it.

Sometimes I dream I have found that neighborhood again, but that's only a dream.

Sisters

We spend the day together on the island. I have never been here before, but it has been my sister's home forever. We sit on the sand, running rivulets of it through our fingers, and gaze across the water at the city while we talk.

"Tell me about your life," my sister urges me, and so I do. I tell her I write poems and that I have written several poems about her. I describe my two children—her niece and nephew—and my son-in-law and grandson. I say that I like to cook and bake. I show her family photographs on my phone.

"How are you?" I ask her.

"All the days are the same," she replies "I sit here most days, unless there is heavy rain, and I look across the water. When it rains, I sit there." She points to a small pavilion with benches ringed by trees and flowers. "I love flowers," she says. "Do you?"

"Yes," I say. "We both inherited that from Mom. She was a great gardener. One year I planted lots of purple flowers and felt vaguely guilty, because she never liked purple rhododendrons, but the flowers looked nice, and I think she would have liked them, too."

"The flowers are lovely here," my sister says. "I especially like the dahlias." She points to them, and I nod.

"I love music the most," I say. "I took piano lessons for many years. When I was a child I took cello lessons, and in high school I taught myself the clarinet and the guitar. Eventually everything faded away except the piano. I practiced every day for an hour or two. Mom also loved music, especially opera and Schubert lieder."

"I love music, too," my sister says. "I listen to it here, but I couldn't learn an instrument."

When evening begins to nibble at the edges of late afternoon, I get up and brush off bits of sand.

"I think I should go now," I say.

"It was wonderful to see you," my sister answers, looking up at me.

"There's one more thing I want to know," I say. "Either I never knew, or I forgot. When is your birthday?"

My sister speaks, but there is a sudden gust of wind, and I can't hear her words. "I can't hear you!" I call, as the wind pushes me away and widens the distance between us. "Never mind!" I yell. "I'm glad we had this day!"

The boat is waiting at the edge of the island, and I climb over its sloped edge and into my assigned seat.

"Strap in," the boat man reminds me, and I do. "Now we are headed to Valhalla. I'm sure you know that people are waiting for you, and that Rachmaninoff is also there. Did you enjoy your day with your sister?"

"Very much," I reply. It is at that moment I realize I know neither her birthdate nor her name. Perhaps my parents hadn't named her, since she was stillborn. She was immediately taken, in the custom of that time, to one of the city islands and buried in an unmarked grave. I was born several years later.

"I was so happy when the hospital called that I cut myself shaving," my father told me many times. "I sang to myself in the mirror: Now I have a daughter! I have a baby girl!"

They are all gone, and now I am gone, too. I will never know my sister's birthday or her name. But I finally saw her, on my journey from the hospital morgue to the cemetery, and I am pleased to know that we both love music and flowers, like our mother did.

Gridlock

"Note my new address," writes Gordon. "I moved to a bigger place. It was bad timing, because the transit workers are on strike, and now I'm miles from the office. If you're coming to Washington, give me a call. Maybe we can get together."

I reread the letter. Does "maybe" mean a twenty-five percent chance or a ninety-five percent chance? Does "get together" mean a cup of coffee or a leisurely candlelight dinner? The only meal Gordon and I ever shared was a hot dog at Port Authority. We hadn't had breakfast, and Gordon said he was hungry. While we ate, I concentrated on making my fingers brush his—not obviously, but not casually either. It took us five bites to finish. Gordon took the mustard-stained wax paper from my hand and threw it into an overflowing trashcan. He checked his watch, and we ran into Port Authority. The line at his gate was already boarding. Gordon paused and kissed me. His lips tasted of mustard and sunlight. Until that kiss, we had never touched. Gordon moved forward, turning once to wave. I waved back and tried to smile.

I make a note of his new address. Is it a new building or an old one? Does he own or rent? Does he live with someone? Will he invite me to his home? In our letters, we write, "I read a great book that you might like," or "I saw a terrific movie." We were in the same creative writing class at college. One day he said, "You write so well. I'm always glad when Professor Sherman chooses one of your poems to read."

We have been writing to each other since graduation. On graduation day, I was standing with my parents. My boyfriend had broken up with me, by telephone, the week before, and I was taking one dazed step after another. My parents were worried about me, but I couldn't find the words to reassure them. The entire world was awash in tears. Gordon came over to ask if he could write to me. I nodded yes, he stood there smiling, and then we waved goodbye.

When one of my poems was published a year after graduation, I wrote to him. I couldn't decide how to sign my letter, so I just signed my name. "That's great!" he replied. He signed his letter "Love." I wrote back to recommend a novel I was reading. He sent me some pages from a journal he was keeping. We kept writing. I hoped he would ask me to visit him.

Then he wrote that he had a job interview in New York, and could he come and stay at my apartment for one night? I still lived with my parents, but they were away on vacation. I said yes. When he rang the doorbell at dinnertime, I didn't recognize him in a suit. He refused dinner, saying that he had been interviewed over an enormous lunch, and I panicked as I wondered what we would do all evening. I poured two glasses of wine the same color as the darkening sky and motioned him toward the sofa. The evening light made the furniture look rich and solid; Gordon, in his dark suit, looked somber and assured, like the kind of man who models expensive watches. I wanted to say something meaningful, but I couldn't find the words. Gordon sipped his wine in silence, his eyes fixed somewhere outside. I watched his hands, which stayed points of light as the room darkened. For the first time since college, longing gusted against my eyes.

"Gordon?" I said. There was no answer. The room was very dark. Perhaps he had dozed off? Perhaps I had? I got up and flicked on a light, slicing the room with a bright band. "What?" asked Gordon, turning to me slightly. "Let me give you a pillow and some blankets," I said. "This sofa's pretty comfortable. I'll come to Port Authority with you tomorrow morning."

"I didn't get the job in New York," wrote Gordon several weeks later, "but I was offered a job in Washington. Thank you for letting me stay at your apartment. I'm going back to college to visit before I start my new job. I'll think of you when I walk past the English Department." I threw the letter in the garbage, and then I took the bottle of wine we had shared and poured the rest of it down the kitchen drain.

Next week I am being sent to Washington. I have had more poems published. I have a job. I have a boyfriend. But part of me still thinks of Gordon. I want it to be graduation day. I want to ask, "Meet me later for a beer?" Although I know we would have changed out of our caps and gowns, I imagine us sitting at the student union in our graduation clothes. I would say: "My boyfriend broke up with me last week. Please come home with me." Then I'd lean across the scarred wooden table and kiss him. These words still beat against my heart, like trapped moths.

Next week I fly to Washington, buckled into my seat to ensure a safe arrival. I have work to do and museums I want to visit.

"Let me come with you," says my boyfriend. "We'll have fun."

"No," I say. "I'll be too busy, and you'll be bored. Let's take a trip together another time." But once I get to Washington, I don't want to be busy. What I want to do is sit in a cab and pretend to be impatient.

"Sorry, lady," the cab driver will say as the meter ticks inexorably, "but the transit drivers are on strike, and it's all gridlock here."

"No problem," I'll say, and I'll turn my attention to the chatter on his radio, grateful for the story of other people's lives.

Effects of Stress

It has been snowing lightly for hours. At 5:30 I set the table and pour myself a glass of wine. Sarah is coming over to dinner at 6:00, and then we are going to the symphony. Yesterday I told her it would be a simple meal, but I didn't mean it. I've been cooking and baking all day; the apartment smells like bread and roasting meat. A little before 6:00 I turn down the burners, lower the oven temperature, and take my glass of wine into the living room. By now the street is thickly covered. The cars look soft, as if they're wrapped in crumpled quilts and topped with white down pillows.

I first spoke to Sarah at last year's office party. I had seen her many times in the hallways, talking to different people. At the party, as she dipped triangular chips into a bowl of guacamole, I watched her graceful hands and admired her delicately carved wedding ring. When I told her I thought that we lived a few blocks from each other, she asked if we could carpool to work.

"We can both save money on gas and keep each other awake," she said. I agreed. I lived in a small, dark apartment that seemed to shrink a little more each week. Every weekend I moved my desk and table and narrow bed around, hoping to create the illusion of space and light, but my furniture remained stolid and glowered from every wall. I lacked the will to move. The chance to spend time with Sarah five days a week was an unexpected gift--I felt less trapped when I was with her. As we carpooled, I told her funny stories, recommended books and music, and brought her pieces of buttered toast to eat as we drove. I wanted her to be my friend.

I had moved to this city to live with my college boyfriend. Our plan was that I would go to graduate school while he was in law school. Then we would get married. Before I arrived, he fell in love with another law student. I saw them together, once, as I walked past a supermarket. He was loading a bag of groceries into a small silver car. That wasn't the car he owned when we were together. He was wearing a bright blue parka, not the navy blue one he had worn in college. He didn't see me. His girlfriend looked incuriously at me, a stranger, as I walked by. I watched how he helped her lift the grocery bags out of the shopping cart, how she smoothed his hair behind his ear, how together they pushed the empty cart to the side of the parking lot—until they drove away.

Willy, Sarah's husband, is a doctoral student in experimental psychology. He studies the effects of stress on rats by overcrowding their cages and feeding them cola drinks and crushed antacid tablets. Some of the rats get so upset that they just lie down and give up. Others, maddened, try to bite Willy. He wears thick gloves when he works with them. At another party, where he and I were the only people not drunk or dancing, we spoke desultorily of my job, his research, and the not-quite-Southern city in which we live. I asked him how his data could be applied to humans, and he said that he couldn't generalize until many more studies had been completed.

We began to argue—or rather, I began to argue, and he tried to explain.

"Of course we can extrapolate some findings," he said apologetically.

"That's not the point," I replied. I felt that what caused stress in rats was not what caused stress in humans. "You're just a rat gastroenterologist. Your experiments have nothing to do with feelings." As he grew more defensive, my anger bloomed. Our conversation ended abruptly. I don't remember the rest of the evening.

Willy and Sarah have been married for six years. At their high school prom, Sarah left her boyfriend and kissed Willy. Once they were living together at college, Willy confessed to her how happy he was when she kissed him, and it was at that moment that he blurted out,

"So will you marry me someday?"

When Sarah told me how Willy and she met, I wanted to ask her how she had the courage to act. I didn't ask. Sarah offers facts, not confidences. As we carpooled, I told her jokes and stories, tried to charm her, imitated people we worked with, and made her laugh.

"Keep your eyes on the road!" she'd say to me. When she drove, she looked straight ahead, shifting gears smoothly. Even the way she stopped at traffic lights implied choice rather than law.

Now things have changed, or maybe we have changed. Neil lives across the street from me. Like Sarah and me, he is an editor. All the English majors in this city pass through the editing department of its one publishing company. Some leave after a few months, and others stay for life. There are more than 30 editors in the office on any ordinary day. At first we all struggle to make medical textbooks understandable to medical students and still hold true to our belief that good writing matters. After a few months, most of us begin to dream of finding a new job. In the evenings Neil writes poetry. He brings in poems to show us. He is blond and thin like Willy, but younger, with a cocky cowboy strut. He stared at Sarah all fall—in the cafeteria, at the copy machine, and at the end of each day. She flirted with him absent-mindedly. She flirts with everyone.

One day in the car she said to me, "Fantasies are more important to me now, but that's normal." I didn't understand what she meant. I thought it had something to do with being married and giving up other choices in life. Maybe that would make fantasies more important.

Before Christmas, Neil left a dark red rose on Sarah's desk during lunch break. It was just beginning to unfold. On the way home she held it carefully, without speaking. I could see her falling in love with him as we drove through the dusk. I wanted to say, "Wait! He's only interested in you because you're older, because you're married, because you're beautiful." But I said nothing. Sarah held the rose to her cheek as I drove.

Sarah, Neil, and I began to ice skate on Sunday mornings. She wanted to be with him. I wanted to be with her. Willy doesn't like to ice skate. "Why be so cold?" he would say. At the rink I would swerve sharply, cutting away from Sarah and Neil so that they could be alone. I didn't like Neil, but Sarah looked happier than I had ever seen her. I imagined that she would be the one person who could do it—love two people and never have to choose, be one person living two lives. Sometimes I thought of my old boyfriend. Sometimes I watched Sarah and Neil. Always, my cheeks were so cold that my tears felt like bee stings.

I look out the window and sip my wine. Sarah's car is parked across the street. I wait for her footsteps in the hall. When none sound, I tell myself that she's listening to the end of a song, putting on her gloves, or combing her hair. After a few more minutes I begin to worry. I open the door to the hall and look out. No one is there. It's after 6:00. Then I close the door and lean my head against it. She's at Neil's. We've been ice-skating for two months. He stared at her all fall. She held the rose so carefully. Her car is wrapped in snow.

I go into the kitchen and take the salad and the butter out of the refrigerator. I turn off the burners and the oven. I slice bread and pour water into goblets. For music, I choose Mendelssohn's *Songs Without Words.* If Sarah arrives in the next five minutes, we can eat quickly and still get to the symphony on time. As I glance up at the clock, the door to the building creaks open. I open the door to my apartment before Sarah knocks. The piano pauses and resumes more delicately. Sarah's eyes look bruised as if she has been crying, but she is smiling. She brushes past me gently, saying,

"I need to take a shower." I give her a white towel. She is late. She has slept with Neil. Everything has changed. I try to say "This isn't possible," but the water is running, the bathroom fan is whirring, my lips cannot form the words, and she was smiling.

"Do you have any lotion?" Sarah calls. I get the lotion from my dresser and stand outside the door. The music continues to fill the air. It is orderly and clear. I feel as if

I can't take a breath. I hear Sarah drop something. My heart is thudding. I lean my head against the wall. Still holding the lotion, I go into the kitchen and look at the clock. I call to Sarah that we can eat and forget about the symphony, or we can forget about dinner and leave now.

"Come in and talk to me while I dry my hair," Sarah replies. I put the lotion back on my dresser and go into the bathroom. Sarah is flushed. She hums to herself as she rubs her hand across the mirror, clearing a circle so that she can see her face. I want to shake her and ignore her at the same time. I ask her where she has been and why she is late. When she says, "At Neil's," with no apology and no explanation, everything changes between us. I think of Willy and his rats. I think of carpooling. I think of the day I transferred all my longing and my dreams for friendship and love from James to Sarah. If I were to look at Sarah now, her eyes would be a cool green, not the inviting hazel I have rested in so often.

I look out the small foggy window. Sarah has cracked it open, and the air is fresh and cold. I put my face near it. The snow has stopped, and now the Mendelssohn ends. I turn to leave, to put on something different –- Bob Dylan warning me not to think twice, or Joni Mitchell crooning about dreams and false alarms — but suddenly I am crying, and Sarah, for the first time, is hugging me. Her hair is damp against my cheek. Her arms are warm. She smells like soap and roses. I press my face into her shoulder and sob. She's saying softly in my ear,

"Everything's fine, don't worry about me, I know what I'm doing"--her voice tentative, as if she's waiting for me to reassure her in turn—and I want to believe her, I want to tell her what she wants to hear, but now I know that everything that's happening is wrong.

Market Day

Today is market day, so after breakfast I'll look around and think about what food I need and what food I want. I've been craving peaches. While I eat a slice of bread I look at my placemat. I sewed six placemats in 2020, when people were told to stay inside. Two placemats are of chickens, two are of birds, and two are of leaves. They all have different color bindings and thread. The stitches are crooked, because I'm not very good at sewing. The craft shelves at the big box stores were picked clean by the time I looked for craft supplies, so I bought whatever I could find. No matter. I like them all. I stroke the chicken placemat and remember a long-ago day with chickens. My husband, our two children, and I stayed overnight at a bed-and-breakfast on an organic potato and blueberry farm, and when we awakened we collected eggs from eight colorful chickens. One chicken had shaggy caramel feathers. Another was sleek and dark red. The innkeeper cooked potato and cheese omelets for us, which we ate on a screened-in porch with a cold green tile floor. The eggs were so fresh that their yolks glowed orange.

I'm done with my bread. I find my tote bag and head out to the market. It's in the center of the city. I can still walk well enough, unlike some people my age who use a cane, but I am careful to go slowly and sit down along the way if necessary. It's not good to get sick or infirm. There are still some benches at the bus stops, but the buses are long gone.

The weather is good. The sun is warm, but the breeze is cool. There are no longer many people out walking, but I nod and smile to the few I see, and they smile and nod back, except for one man who is arguing with himself and does not see me. When I get to the market I go inside, to the sign-in table, and add my name to the ledger. Next to my name I write that I am looking for peaches first and any other stone fruit as an alternate. If you are older than 75, which I am, you are excused from the digital world. Otherwise, you are provided with a new mobile device every year that you must carry everywhere and use for everything.

"Please wait over there until your name is called," says the young woman behind the table. She looks at the ledger and enters my name into her mobile device. She points to a row of chairs against one wall.

"Yes, thank you," I say. I walk over to the chairs and sit down. Sometimes I bring a book with me to pass the time, but I didn't today. There are no libraries anymore, but I have made my own books last. I don't mind rereading them, just as I don't mind replaying the few music CDs I still own. I don't know what I'll do when my ancient Bose CD player breaks down. Sing or hum the music to myself, I suppose.

It is not too long before my name is called. I am pointed toward a table where a young woman and a girl stand behind several baskets.

"Good morning," I say.

"Good morning," the woman replies. She is sunburned, slim, maybe in her late thirties. Her arms and hands look strong. Her face looks tired. The girl is perhaps seven or eight. She leans against her mother and smiles. She has auburn hair and a chipped front tooth.

"I had hair your color when I was your age," I tell her.

"Did you like it?" she asks. "Or did you get teased? The boys make fun of me because I have red hair."

"I was teased me, too," I say, although in my case two girls teased me. Nancy and Francine. Nancy was meaner, small and bow-legged, with a scrunched-up pug face. Francine was tall and thin, with dandelion hair. One day she showed me how to sew an extra seam along the inside of my jeans to make the legs narrower. That was the style in fourth grade.

"Don't tell Nancy I helped you," she whispered.

Sharing that memory with this girl won't help either of us.

"I always liked my red hair, no matter what anyone said," I tell the girl. "I like your red hair. And I like your freckles. See? I have some freckles too." I point to my nose and am rewarded with another chipped-tooth smile. I smile back.

"I've been craving peaches," I say to the woman. She tilts one of her baskets toward me. I see white peaches, which I like even more than the yellow ones.

"They're freestone. Organic. I use the old farming methods."

"I'll take as many as you will give me for one memory," I say. "It's from thirty or thirty-five years ago. Is that OK?" She nods yes. I begin to talk. I tell her and her daughter that my husband and I and our two children drove out one muggy July weekend to stay overnight at a bed and breakfast at an organic farm. I tell them that we were on our way to an amusement park, but the drive there and back was too long to do in one day. The farm, near the amusement park, advertised pick-your-own organic potatoes and blueberries, which I thought my children would enjoy, and they did, but they loved the chickens and the small pond with a snapping turtle more. There was a friendly Sheltie dog named Connie that frisked around our legs. I used to have a photograph of my children with their arms around that dog.

"The chickens were not the usual kind," I said. "These chickens had shaggy feathers and were glorious colors like caramel and deep red. But they clucked and chattered like regular chickens. When we tried to take their eggs, they tried to peck us. But we gathered the eggs and took them inside to the innkeeper. He cooked us potato and cheese omelets. We ate those omelets at a big wood table in a screened-in porch with a tiled floor. The floor was green, like the ocean. It felt cold on our bare feet, but it was summer, and the air was warm, so the floor felt good." The woman and the girl listened, nodding.

"I can see the chickens!" the girl said. "Did they have names?"

"Yes, they did," I say. "The shaggiest one was named Dulce de Leche. There was a popular caramel ice cream in stores that year, and the chicken was named after the ice cream. The red chicken was named Red. The white one was named Marshmallow." None of this is true. The chickens did not have names. My daughter, who loved dulce de leche ice cream, named the shaggy chicken as she chased after it, calling "Wait for me, Dulce de Leche! Wait for me!" Of course, the chicken just ran faster. We laughed about it until it was replaced by other, newer memories. I don't mind embellishing this memory for this girl.

"And then we left the farm and went to an amusement park. But that could be a memory for another day." I don't think about the amusement park often. It was expensive and noisy, filled with loud rude people, and the lines were very long.

"Take as many peaches as you can carry in your bag," the woman tells me. I thank her and fill my tote bag.

"Good-bye," I say. I begin the walk home. I'll use most of the peaches to make peach jam. I'll eat the rest. I think about the organic farm. I know that my memory of that weekend at the organic farm will fade slowly over the next few hours, until it is gone. I think of it once more as I walk, and then I tell it good-bye. It's better to leave a memory before it leaves you.

Something happened to people's memories after the pandemic. No one knows why. People spent so much time online then. They had to. There were virtual meetings to attend, appointments to keep, and assignments to complete. Maybe it wasn't all the screen time, though. Maybe it was something in the water, or the soil, or the food combined with the screen time. Maybe it was the virus. Maybe it was the politics. Nobody knew. Nobody knows. What we know is that one year, people younger than fifty became unable to remember anything that had happened more than a year earlier. I don't know what I would do without my memories, especially because now they are the only thing I have to barter. The financial system and the old social safety nets crumbled years ago, and elderly people must use their memories and their skills to barter for food and assistance. I'll give some peach jam to my neighbor, and he will repair my broken window.

I pick and choose which memories to give away. I give away only ones I can afford to lose. Yes, the weekend at the organic farm was fun, but I have other memories of my husband and children. I have other memories of peaches and kitchens and cooking and farms. As I walk home, I think about a summer when I was younger than the red-haired girl at the market. I'm in the kitchen of my grandmother's summer home. It's July, and very hot, and the table is covered with a a red-and-white oilcloth laden with cut-up peaches and peach juice. My mother and father found bushels and bushels of overripe peaches for sale and brought them home. My grandmother is canning peaches and making peach jam so that we can eat peaches all through the winter. I'm watching her. My mother is in and out of the kitchen, telling me to be careful around the paring knife and the boiling water and to be a good girl and stay out of my grandmother's way. My father is in the living room, fixing something. My brother is playing with toys near my father.

"OK, Mommy," I say. "I'll be careful."

My grandmother smiles at me and slips me another slice of ripe peach to eat. It's so sweet, like a slice of sun.

Although I'm not tired, I sit down at one of the bus stop benches. I take a peach out of my tote bag and hold it between my hands. It's perfect. I take a bite.

Lemon Meringue
and Something Else

Last year I visited the city in which we became friends, and I tried to find that pie place you took me to once, all those years ago. I couldn't find it. It must have closed. I never knew its address, only that it was west of the expressway. I got off at every exit, muttering to myself that it had to be somewhere, even if somewhere was east of the sun and west of the moon. I wanted to find it and order four slices of pie and eat them with two forks—a bite for you, and a bite for me, the flavors intermingling on our tongues and reminding us of all the meals we shared. I can see that pie place as clearly as I can see you and me, young and intense and full of plans for our lives, gesticulating wildly as we talked too loudly in the small booth with its cracked red vinyl benches and blaring 60s music. We were so young, with huge tortoiseshell glasses that were the style back then, and long, curly hair that we parted in the middle and tried to brush straight, and carefully frayed bell-bottom blue jeans. People sometimes mistook us for each other, but it was only because we both wore glasses and had curly hair. I can still taste the lemon meringue, coconut custard, and blueberry pie we ordered, but there's one thing I can't remember, and now there are two questions I want to ask you. What was the second pie you ordered that we shared, and is there pie in the sky when you die?

The last time I saw you was more than thirty years ago. You took me to that restaurant that served only pie, somewhere west of the expressway.

"They have two dozen kinds, and they're all homemade," you told me as you drove.

"The place has no name, but I call it Pie in the Sky. It's so great! What kind of pies are you going to order?"

"Lemon meringue and something else," I said. "Probably coconut custard."

"I'll get blueberry and something else," you said. "Then we can share."

Our husbands tolerated our friendship and socializing with good humor, often leaving the dinner table to talk or watch television while we exchanged recipes and shared our dreams, and then they were summoned back and thanked for their absence and patience with homemade carrot cake (you) and lemon meringue pie (me) for dessert. We both liked to cook. Whenever we left work for a quick pizza lunch offsite, you gave me your cornmeal-dusted pizza crusts, and I gave you the cheese-laden points of my slices.

"A perfect friendship," we agreed. It was. Only once did we talk about making our friendship something else, and we kissed once, but that was all. We were so young, and everything in life seemed possible, but we must have known that everything in life is never possible. Neither of us wanted to ruin our marriages and, quite possibly, our friendship, and so we exchanged one tentative kiss, smiled awkwardly, said "That was nice," and went on with our marriages. Neither of us mentioned that kiss again.

Our friendship was a good thing. Do all good things come to an end, or is that just a saying? I wish I could ask you. After a few years in that city, my husband and I moved east and had three daughters, and soon after we moved your husband and you split up. You met and married your second husband, who had a son from a previous marriage, and the three of you moved west. In those days before e-mail, we wrote letters often and called sometimes and sent birthday gifts for several years, until we didn't. Then, my only news of you was news from friends of friends of friends. They told me you were working here or there and that you and your family were fine. And then I heard that you weren't fine. I wrote to you right away, and you replied immediately.

"I'm doing as well as can be expected," you wrote. "People have been so kind. A nerve block eased the pain. I actually don't mind not having long hair anymore. Remember how we used to try to brush out our curls? Now I love my curly wisps."

Again, I wrote back right away, but you didn't answer, and a few months later I heard you were dead. Why didn't I call you? That was eight years ago. It will never seem real.

Refinishing

I refinish fine furniture carefully, at a good price. My specialty is wardrobes. Early on I advertised, but now it's all word of mouth. Because I work onsite and people have children and pets, I invented a nontoxic stripping agent that smells like cinnamon and oranges. When I was a child, we didn't have real furniture. We had veneer-topped particleboard. We had a falling-down house with snuffling kids, cold, noise, dirt, a thieving father who drank a lot and hit all of us, and a mother who should have left him but wouldn't or couldn't. I did pretty well in school, but what I liked best was reading fairy tales at the library. In my favorite, a child taps on the back of a closet and steps into another world. That's why I work onsite. Once I'm gone, I won't be accused of stealing anything.

Runs Like a Dream

"I'm so glad you're here," I say, turning my head toward my parents in the back seat. "How do you like my new car? I love it."

"I was worried it was one of those SUVs," my mother says. "I hear they can tip over."

"No, it's a regular sedan," I say. "It's just a little higher off the ground than most sedans. Remember that blue Rambler you had when I was in kindergarten?"

My father groans. "That car never missed an opportunity to break down at the worst moment. Remember when we were on our way to New England and it broke down on the Thruway?"

"The green Plymouth that came after it wasn't much better," my mother remarked.

"I learned to drive on that Plymouth," I said, as I put my blinker on and prepare to turn left. "When I braked, I felt as if my foot needed to go through the floor to stop the car. Hey, look out the right window after I make this turn. Remember how that used to be nothing but fields? That peach farm was there. Now it's built up. Too built up." We agree that the area has become very crowded.

"Remember where we bought raspberries? We'd buy as many boxes as they'd give us and make jam to last all winter. They built the county complex on that farm. Look out your left window." My parents look out and murmur that they remember the farm and the raspberries. We drive in comfortable silence on an access road that parallels the highway.

"This road probably *was* the highway before they built the highway," I say, as I put on my blinker and turn the car toward home. "I like it. I wish I could drive everywhere on an access road alongside a highway, not on the highway itself. Everyone goes too fast." I slip in a CD. "You know this one, Mom. It's Rachmaninoff. The elegiac piano trios. Remember? I can never decide which one I like best, so I've decided I like both of them the best." We drive some more. I point out new and old sites. My parents listen, nod, and comment. The music plays. The CD is almost over when I pull into the garage. I wait until the last notes fade, eject the CD, turn off the engine, and gather my belongings from the front passenger seat.

"OK, you two," I say. "It's so wonderful to see you." I get out and peer inside the car before I go into the house to start dinner. Of course, there's no one in the back seat. I know that. My mother and father rode in this car once, many years ago, when it was new. If they were alive today, my father would be 104 and my mother 96. I never know when they will arrive to travel with me, in my car, again. My friends and coworkers tease me about my car all the time.

"You're still driving that old car?" they ask, laughing or surprised. "What century is it from?"

"Yes," I say. "I'm still driving it. It has a CD player. It runs like a dream. I don't ever want to say good-bye."

Video Taylor

Taylor usually doesn't stick around after book club. She gets up, murmuring an apology for not staying to chat, and leaves. Today, as she pulls her jacket from the back of the chair, the other three women begin to talk about vacations.

"Tell us next week if you and Matt are going anywhere!" Miranda calls after her.

"I will!" Taylor calls back.

After book club, Taylor usually picks up a few groceries. If she doesn't need anything, she drives to the diner for coffee and a corn muffin before going home. Taylor bakes better muffins than the diner does, and she makes better coffee, but she likes to sit in a booth meant for four people as waitresses bustle by. Once in a while Taylor goes out with the other women for lunch, and she has nothing against any of them, really, but they are friends of proximity, not friends of her heart.

"Be glad this town has a good library and a book club and three other women who like to read," she tells herself, dipping pieces of muffin into her coffee. She thinks about the two novels she chose for book club—*Same As It Ever Was* and *Signal Fires*. She doesn't know if the other women liked the two books as much as she did, but no one complained. Taylor doesn't always like the books other women choose, but she reads and discusses their choices and patiently waits her turn to choose another book.

"Be glad," she repeats, taking out her wallet. "It could be worse." She leaves a generous tip for the waitress, because difficult as her job at the advertising agency is, she doesn't have to be on her feet carrying heavy trays and smiling. The default expression at the agency is a scowl, at least between the creative department and everyone else. Anyway, she's finally part time and partially remote, ever since she threatened to quit on the spot during a particularly difficult product launch, when every client demand triggered an agency-wide existential crisis about fonts and colors and line breaks and calls to action.

Taylor calls home on the landline that she keeps meaning to cancel, but no one picks up.

"Heading home," she says after the beep. "I'll make something for lunch, and then we can walk." She has lived in this rural-suburban township, with its clogged, coiled highways and warring box stores and chain restaurants, for so long that she doesn't see it anymore. Where the diner sits, across from the ever-expanding hospital, was once a cherry farm and then parched land on which real estate and political signs came and went.

Sitting in her car, Taylor thinks, "I could watch the video now, on my phone," but it's not satisfying on a small screen. She drives home. Living here was supposed to be temporary, a place for Taylor and Matt to have easy commutes to jobs they hate and are grateful to have, a place for Jeremy to go to a safe and good-enough public school. How can a wife with a degree in studio art and a husband with a degree in philosophy afford the city? Their studio apartment barely fit their double bed, let alone Taylor's art supplies and canvases. When she became pregnant, they moved here because they couldn't afford anything closer to the city. They vowed to save money and move back to the city, already changed since their graduate-school days, now almost unrecognizable, but still the city, their city, where they were born, had parents, had friends; where they can walk everywhere and not own a car, where they can go to museums and concerts; where asking for apples other than Red Delicious and Granny Smith at the supermarket does not elicit a befuddled stare. Who knew that a child and a tiny house could cost so much?

"What did we do wrong?" Matt asks often.

"We did nothing wrong and we did everything wrong," Taylor thinks. "How can anyone parse every decision?"

"We did nothing wrong," she says. It's better to avoid these conversations with Matt, who has been morose since being laid off from his job at a nonprofit. Taylor could never quite grasp what the organization did, let alone what Mark's responsibilities were. What mattered was he could cover her on his health insurance if she lost her job.

"I'm almost 62," he says. "No one is going to hire me. I'll just take early retirement and get on Social Security."

Taylor makes sandwiches for herself and Matt.

"Where's Jeremy?"

"Doing an extra shift at the liquor store."

Jeremy is home again after cycling through a variety of minimum-wage jobs and shared apartments. Taylor wants him to go back to school and get a degree in something useful, but Jeremy resists. "What's the point?" he says. "There are no good jobs unless you want to be in tech, which I don't." Now he works three part-time jobs to pay for his high-deductible health care insurance plan that doesn't pay for anything but a yearly physical.

Matt inhabits the sofa and reads history books.

"You'll like this book," he tells Taylor whenever he starts a new book. She always opens the book and pretends to read a paragraph or two.

"It looks interesting, but I just like fiction better, thank you. Let's go to the library whenever you want more books." Taylor used to choose books for Matt after book club, but Mark's therapist said it's better if Matt does things for himself whenever possible. They eat lunch. Taylor's phone pings.

"I need to do some work after lunch," she says, reading the text message. "They moved up a deadline. Surprise, surprise! I have to finalize a brochure. Let's walk after I do that, OK?"

Matt nods.

Taylor heads upstairs to the narrow third bedroom she imagined would be her art studio but is now her office and a storage room, and turns on her laptop. The client wants the colors sharpened, some illustrations moved around, and some fonts changed. Taylor makes the changes and hits *Send*, glad that the client didn't want the entire brochure redone this late in the project.

She hesitates, then clicks on the YouTube video a co-worker sent her a few months ago. It's only 14 minutes long. Matt will read for twice that long before wondering where she is. Taylor clicks *Play* and watches as a large family gathers to celebrate parties, graduations, weddings, and vacations during one year. Each person looks into the camera and rhapsodizes about a specific relative, friend, vacation, wedding, or celebration.

"I saw you in a video! You have such wonderful friends and relatives!!" her co-worker said. "Who made the video? Your son? A sister? A friend? You guys do such wonderful things all the time! What a great group of people!"

Taylor starts to say, "It's not me. It's a different Taylor," but instead hears herself saying, "Isn't it great? I don't remember who made it, but thank you! I like it too. And, yes, we are a very busy group of friends and family."

Taylor knows that Video Taylor, who does look uncannily like her, and Video Taylor's friends and family must have problems too, that this is a video, that everyone is performing for the camera and probably begins sulking or arguing with one or more people as soon as the video is over. Or maybe even during it, in the background. Still, the video has some kind of hold on her. Taylor finds watching it more relaxing than coherent breathing, which her doctor suggested she try when she can't fall back asleep at night or during long and hostile client meetings on Zoom. Now she watches the video once, twice, humming along, pretending to be Video Taylor, her friends at her side, her three children next to her, her dead parents and grandparents and aunts and uncles alive and nearby, looking at her proudly, and her husband employed and happy and smiling, his arms wrapped around her.

"Hi, everyone," Taylor says, smiling. She waves to the screen.

"Are you coming down soon?" Matt calls.

"In a minute! Just finishing up," Taylor replies, her finger hovering over the *Play* button. She thinks that she could sit here forever.

Longing Time

My grandmother lived with us one summer. Every afternoon, as she sat in her rocking chair and crocheted, I sat on the floor while she told me the same story.

"In 1913, my sister Irina and I fled our home because war was coming. We went to Holland. From there we planned to sail to England and then to America. In Holland, an Army officer fell in love with Irina, and she with him. They got married and stayed in Holland. I boarded the ship alone. We waved good-bye until we couldn't see each other anymore. In America I married your grandfather." Her hand stroked my hair. Her hair had once been red, like mine. "I still miss her so much."

The sisters hadn't seen each other since they waved goodbye. They wrote letters and spoke on the phone. Both were afraid to fly. That summer, while my grandmother stayed with us, my brother played as usual with his toys. My mother banged pots and pans in the kitchen. My father went to work. I listened to my grandmother. Sometimes I'd rest my head on her knee, so I didn't have to see the odd look on her face. I didn't know what to call it. Then she'd rub my head, give thanks that I had inherited her red hair, and tie a red ribbon around my wrist to ward off evil.

I thought living in Holland would be better than living in America. In my book about Dutch children, they skated to school on the river. Their round faces were untroubled.

"Why do I have to skate in circles?" I complained as my mother laced up my skates at the public rink.

Years later, I know what to call that look on my grandmother's face. I call it Longing Time. I'm in Longing Time when I skate. I go to the rink Monday through Friday. I teach history at the high school, and the last bell rings at 2:29. By 2:45, I'm at the rink. My husband works the evening shift. Our daughter is at college.

I got married half my life ago. There still are days I want to run away. In the car, when a wistful song plays, I want to keep driving. I never did. I never do. My husband loves me. I love him. He's a wonderful man. We love our daughter. I have friends. I have hobbies. I've never broken anybody's heart. There were some years when I poured myself wine the minute I came home, or watched television all evening, but then I started skating again and didn't need to do those things anymore.

At first, one of the attendants at the rink was amused. He smirked at me. I could tell what he was thinking: "Why does a middle-aged woman need those fancy skates?" Then, without any effort, I outpaced him on the rink. I can cut through any configuration of people. He watched me the entire time. Afterwards, he asked me where I learned to skate like that.

"Holland," I said. "I'm Dutch. I skated to school on the river every morning." I was born here in the States, but he doesn't have to know that. Now he waves hello and good-bye. Sometimes he gives me extra time on the ice, before the Zamboni comes out to clean. I don't know his name. I don't know anything about him. He's young, like Stephen and I were when we met in graduate school.

When I skate, I think of Stephen. I used to think of him all the time. That was a mistake.

"What's wrong?" my husband would ask.

"Nothing," I'd say, as I chopped onions and sobbed. "Nothing's wrong. It's the onions." First, I think of Stephen as the beautiful, heartless boy who left me for someone else. Then I think of him as he is now—married to his third wife. "This won't work if either of us gets greedy," he cautions me, the few times we've talked on the phone. Then we talk about meeting, although we haven't met. We just talk in circles about it.

My grandmother entered a nursing home when I was in college. Several times she decided to fly to Holland, but she always changed her mind. Then her sister died. When I called Stephen, after all those years of longing for him, it was my grandmother's face I saw as I dialed his number. After Irina died, my grandmother turned her face to the wall. I leaned my head against her hand, but she stayed motionless. I still have her red hair, but it is turning gray. Under my sleeve I sometimes wear a red ribbon—but it's to ward off sadness, not evil.

Today the rink is empty. Spring is coming. People are buying mulch and planting flowers. My students groan and fidget. They don't want to be in history class. "Who needs the past?" their expressions shout. When the bell rings, they fly from their seats. Yesterday, I heard birds outside the bedroom window.

"Listen!" I said to my husband. He continued sleeping, one arm flung across me.

It's lovely outside. Inside, everything is frozen. I lace up my skates and look at the attendant. He waves his ungloved hand at me. In graduate school, Stephen waited for me at the rink, his shoulders hunched against the cold. His dark hair fell across his face, but I could see him smiling. I think he did love me. Near the end of every afternoon, as I skate more slowly, that's what I tell myself: "He did love me. He just loved someone else more."

Stephen would wave his ungloved hand. "Come on! It's too cold in here! Let's go someplace warm!" I would skate to him and throw my arms around him. He always felt so warm.

"OK," I'd say. I would have followed him anywhere. That was a whole other time, when I believed life was a straight line. I thought I would travel it in one piece. I thought I would travel it with Stephen.

I lace my skates, stand up, and skate toward the attendant. He's watching me. I won't get any pleasure out of breaking his heart, but I need to see if I can do it.

"What's your name?" I ask him.

The Rosemary Years

Rosemary was my father's fourth wife, but she believed she was his second. She never knew that my father married a woman named Lorraine right after my mother left him, before he married Rosemary. After a a year of marriage to my father, Lorraine took the baby and left for Florida, where she had family. Then it was just my father and me on the weekends, living in a cold-water attic flat. My room must have been a closet, since it was very small and didn't have a window. During the week I lived with my mother and stepfather Frank and my new baby sister, and on the weekends I stayed with my father in his rented attic room.

My mother and father stayed married for seven years, until my mother chose a new husband who liked cleanliness, new possessions, and predictability. I was five or six then. Frank wanted a child to replace the son his first wife took with her when she left. Frank told me that because I was his stepson, I could never be his real son, but that I could live in his home on weekdays until I was sixteen, as mandated by the court.

Every Friday evening my father's ancient, rust-splotched car rattled at the curb outside my mother's neat, well-bleached home, where I waited near the front door with my plastic bag of clothes and toothbrush. Every Sunday evening he dropped me off, again at the curb, and

I trudged inside. The house my mother lived in was small, but it had a large yard. I was sent outside often. I became good at identifying clouds. My half-sister Jeanette, who didn't kick the wall with muddy shoes or yell and lash out, was allowed to stay inside with her toys. In the summers I was expected to be outside all day, so when I was old enough to cross the avenue I walked to the supermarket to gulp in chilled air. Every few weeks, after I was yelled at more often than usual, or was told too many times by Frank that I had a fat face and was full of crap because my eyes were brown and not blue like his and Jeanette's and his real son's eyes, I'd set off for the Wild West or for China with whatever spare change I found between the sofa cushions. After a few blocks, tired and thirsty and unsure how to get from my life to another life, I'd go home. No one ever noticed I'd been gone.

I was thirteen when my father met and married Rosemary. She lived in the leafy suburbs of our small midwestern city with her daughter and twin sons, my newest brothers and sister. Her husband had died young, two years earlier.

"Cancer," my father said, not interested in the specifics. "Let's not tell Rosemary about Lorraine and her baby," my father also said, his arm heavy on my shoulders, right before he introduced me to Rosemary. "It'd make her feel bad. Let's keep them our secret, son."

"Who are Lorraine and her baby?" I asked.

"That woman I was married to for a year after your mother was stolen. Her baby was named Jerry." That Frank stole my mother was still my father's common refrain, although the frequency with which he broadcast it had weakened. Other refrains were that the neighbors were after him and all cashiers were cheating him.

"OK," I said. I attended the wedding, uncomfortable in a shiny blue suit that was too small. Now my father lived in Rosemary's house, which was his house too. I was there only on the weekends, but when I turned sixteen I could live there all the time, if I wanted to. I wanted to. The first time I saw Rosemary's house and her three children, I thought I had died and gone to heaven. The house smelled like oranges and fresh air. There were reclining chairs with cushions and a glass table on the deck, and a fireplace and a picture window in the living room. There was a glossy piano in the den, paintings on the walls, and bookshelves crammed with photographs and pottery as well as books. The kitchen had a dishwasher and a double sink with a garbage disposal. Fresh fruit ripened in a glazed yellow bowl on the kitchen table. Flowers bloomed in a tall green vase in the foyer. Rosemary's children were polite to me. This was the suburbs in the 1960s. I loved it.

Until I turned sixteen, I endured weekdays with my mother, Frank, and Jeannette.

"Get the mayonnaise off the table!" Frank snapped. He didn't like it and didn't want to look at it. I loved mayonnaise. My mother fried his bacon and eggs to leather and sprayed cleaning products above his head before turning down the volume on the television.

"Turn it up!" he said.

"It's too loud already!" She had given him a child. He had given her cars, appliances, and predictability. He went to work each day and deflated into his armchair when he returned. My mother never talked to me about my father, but from my weekends with him, I could see that life with Frank was calmer and cleaner.

On weekends, my father often said, "I'm going out for a couple of hours. Watch some television and eat some pie." He'd point to a half-priced, partially frozen, soon-to-expire supermarket pie sagging on the kitchen counter. Other times he stayed inside the room and sent me out to play. Once, an elderly woman in the building ran a bath for me. I must have been seven or eight.

"You poor boy," she said as the water turned muddy brown. "Doesn't anyone take care of you? Go on, use more soap. Here's a towel to dry off when you're clean." After the water drained, the bathtub contained an inch of dirt. I remember how soft the towel was, like I imagined a cloud would be.

Now I spent my weekends in suburban comfort. Rosemary's husband's will specified that the mortgage be paid and money set aside for college for his three children if he died, so the house was Rosemary's, free and clear, and her children could go to any college they could get into. My father had no objection to living in a four-bedroom ranch house in the suburbs as long as he didn't have to buy the house and pay the taxes and the mortgage, and he didn't object to anyone's going to college as long as he didn't have to pay the tuition. I knew I'd be going to the state university and taking out loans to afford even that.

My first weekend there, all of us standing in the yard, my father briskly rubbed his hands together and said loudly, to no one in particular,

"It's very nice here, isn't it? We're like that movie with the two families and all those kids, aren't we?" Rosemary's children looked at him, unblinking.

"That's twelve children," said Susan, Rosemary's daughter. "We're just four children."

"Twelve, four, what does it matter? Family—that's the most important thing," my father said. This from the man who made me order from the $2 menu rather than the $3 menu at the local greasy spoon on the rare occasions he wasn't creating hamburger patties that were eighty percent breadcrumbs and ketchup. This from the man who wouldn't let my mother buy potatoes if they weren't on sale, when she was pregnant with me, which was the one thing she shared with me about her years with him.

"We're all going to get along just fine. Aren't we, son?" I didn't answer. After some minutes when no one spoke, Susan said to me,

"Do you want to go to the pool?"

"Sure," I said. "But I don't have a bathing suit." The twins, Sammy and Steve, found one of their bathing suits for me. Bathing suits were one more thing my father didn't deem necessary. The one time he and I went on a vacation, we swam in the motel pool in our underwear until the clerk told us to get out.

"Wait a minute," Rosemary said. She darted into the house and returned with suntan lotion and towels, plus a tote bag full of potato chips, oranges, and bottled water.

"Have fun and be careful," she said, giving each of her children a kiss and tousling my hair. "You'll like the pool, Danny."

I liked her already. She was kind as well as pretty. My mother was prettier than Rosemary, but she was never kind. She spent her days cleaning while the television blared soap-opera intrigue through gusts of bleach.

"They tell me at the supermarket that I'm so pretty," my mother would sing, whenever Frank or Jeanette or I asked her a question, twirling in front of the television with her can of Lysol spray.

How did my father convince Rosemary to marry him? How did he fool her into thinking he was normal? He was handsome, so that must have helped, and he could be courtly toward women in an old-fashioned way—holding doors open with a bow, insisting on carrying heavy bags of groceries, that kind of thing. Rosemary must have been lonely. At age 40, with three children and the thought of so many husband-less years unspooling ahead of her, she probably wasn't thinking clearly. My father and Rosemary met at Rosemary's church, at a social event for widowed and divorced parents. My father didn't belong to a specific church. He went wherever eligible women could be found, cycling through all the Christian denominations and occasionally branching out to Unitarianism and the Quakers.

"The pool was great," I told Susan as we walked home. Susan told me about her family.

"Rosemary was named for her two grandmothers, Rose and Mary," she said. "And then she was put in the dead baby basket right after she was born, because she wasn't breathing and the doctor thought she was dead. Then the nurse saw her chest move and yelled, 'This baby's still alive!' And the doctor ran back and took my mom out of the dead baby basket and gave her to her mother, my grandmother." I thought about that. I didn't know what to say. Susan didn't seem to mind that I was silent. We walked together. Sammy and Steve ran off ahead. Then Susan slipped her hand through mine and said, "I'm glad you're my new brother."

"I'm glad too," I said. I pinched myself. Was any of this real?

Things were good for a few years. I often felt that I was living inside a dream. I looked forward to my weekends there. My father and Rosemary took up hobbies that Rosemary thought of—wine making, bread baking, square dancing at the community center. My father participated without complaining too much. I spent the summers with my father, and we four children were sent to Rosemary's parents' farm in the southern part of the state.

"You'll learn how to milk a cow, son," my father told me. This from a man who had never seen one and bought powdered milk because it cost less. Being on the farm wasn't bad, though. We worked hard every day, but we ate pies and cinnamon buns for breakfast and fresh corn and tomatoes at dinner. There was a swimming hole and a tire swing. I did learn how to milk a cow after many tries, and I was proud of myself for not giving up. I developed muscles and grew to my full height. I kissed a girl for the first time. That summer I saw that there were different kinds of people in the world and that life didn't always have to be as mean-spirited or horrible as my parents made it.

When did the cracks in my father's and Rosemary's marriage appear? I think I was eighteen. I was living with them all the time by then and was a senior in high school. After so many years of treating me like a frog and Jeanette like a princess, my mother cried when I announced that I would be living with my father and Rosemary during the week instead of with her and Frank.

"This is your home!"

I'm not sure why she expected me to choose otherwise, but she always liked Hollywood endings, or maybe my moving out would look bad to the neighbors.

"That high school is better, Mom," I said wearily. "I need to do well enough to get a scholarship so I can go to a good college. After college I want to go to journalism school. I'm sure Frank doesn't want to pay my tuition, does he?" That ended the conversation, because Frank didn't. My mother and Frank believed, despite all evidence to the contrary, that my father was Midas, sitting on pots of gold, first in his attic room and later in Rosemary's home without a mortgage.

Every week Rosemary made a big Sunday lunch after church. Often my paternal grandfather was invited, although he had an ulcer from his years as a World War I prisoner and ate only rice or noodles. During one visit, Rosemary asked, "What's wrong with your son? Why can't he act normally?" My grandfather was puzzled. He didn't know what to say, except, "He has a job. He goes to work and comes home." Rosemary stopped talking, perhaps realizing that there was no answer. My father was who he was because he wanted to be, or because he couldn't help being himself, or both. Now I think he would be diagnosed with a condition that could perhaps be treated or managed, but back then there was no diagnosis and therefore no treatment. My father sat there, listening to Rosemary berate him to his father, a politely vacant look on his face.

"Are there any more of these potatoes?" he asked. Rosemary put down her fork and left the table.

Around that time my father started complaining.

"You kids are too noisy! You spend too much money! You never listen to me." That it wasn't his money or his kids, except for me, didn't occur to him. He didn't like the music we played, or our long hair and raggedy bellbottoms, or the television shows we watched. Sammy, Steve, and I kept our heads down and completed our college applications. While we waited for acceptance or rejection letters, Susan turned sixteen. She had been asking for a bikini to replace her one-piece bathing suit, but Rosemary was not amenable to that. My father gave her a bathing suit for her birthday. It was a modest two-piece, not a bikini, but it was still a two piece, and it had a nice geometric pattern in pinks and purples, Susan's favorite colors. Susan liked it.

"Thank you!" she said. "I'll wear it the first time we all go to the pool," she said. Later that month Susan proudly jumped into the water in her new bathing suit, which immediately dissolved. Susan screamed. Rosemary screamed. My father had bought the bathing suit at some fly-by-night budget store, and it wasn't waterproof or water resistant. It was made of some material that dissolved when wet and was probably meant as a gag gift.

"I didn't know!" my father said over and over. "I thought it was a real bathing suit!" The price tag must have been right. When the price was right, nothing else mattered. Poor Susan. Her brothers and I ran over to her with towels, and she wrapped herself in them before getting out of the pool, grabbing her clothes, and stalking off to the changing room.

"Cheapskate," she hissed at my father as she passed him. I'm sure he viewed that as a compliment.

Was that bathing suit the beginning of the end? Was it when Rosemary berated my father to my grandfather? When she opened all the paint cans in the basement and swung paint onto the floor and walls? When she poured chocolate chips into an empty aspirin bottle and swallowed the contents in one gulp in front of him? Was it the evening when my father pulled into the driveway and she threw all the dinner plates at his windshield? Soon after that evening,

Soon after, Rosemary began divorce proceedings. The boys and I went off to our respective colleges.

Rosemary sold the house and rented an apartment for herself and Susan until Susan went away to college. During my college years I would spend a few days in the summers with my mother and Frank and Jeanette, where my mother pretended we were a happy family of four. One summer I ran into Sammy at the movies, and he told me that Rosemary had married a widower and moved with him to the southwest corner of the state, where her parents still lived.

"It's so good to see you, man," Sammy said, sticking out his hand.

"You, too," I said, taking his hand and shaking it. "Give Rosemary and Steve and Susan my best. And my best to you." I meant it. Those years with Rosemary and her three children were the best years of my life.

I didn't exactly lose touch with my father, because he kept contacting me. I just stopped answering his calls when we lived in the same city. Once I got married and moved away, He was too cheap to call long distance. He wrote sometimes, and I threw out his letters. All the letters said was, "You Must Accept Me as Your Father!!!!" in two-inch blocky print. From the return address, I saw that my father was once again living in the city. Whether he owned or rented, worked or was retired, was married or single, I did not know and did not care. I lived a thousand miles away with my wife, near her parents. Over the years, my father's letters came less frequently and finally not at all. Finally I was older than the father I remembered during the Rosemary years.

Then he sent a change-of-address card. He had bought a house near Rosemary's old house. He must have been in his late sixties by then.

"What do you make of this?" I asked my wife and my in-laws. We were sitting on our screened-in porch, enjoying the spring air. No one answered. My wife shrugged. She had never met my father, but I had described him and complained about him and wept because of him so well and so often for so many years that she felt she knew all she wanted to know about him. My father-in-law busied himself with the newspaper. My mother-in-law jumped up to refill our seltzer glasses. They were matter-of-fact, practical people, like my wife, and they viewed my childhood with sadness, distaste, and suspicion—a topic best avoided. They and my wife generally excused my moodiness, my periodic sadness, and my inability to reach my full potential at any job, be it too hard or too easy for me. I now worked as a proofreader for a local newspaper, having been demoted from reporter to copyeditor to proofreader after too many arguments with sources, authors, and coworkers. Proofreading was going OK. I merely had to compare one version of something against another. I could do that. My in-laws, wife, and I sat in silence, listening to the newspaper rustle and the ice cubes clink.

"That's what I think, too," I said. I tore the card in half and stuffed it into my pocket to throw away later..

A few years after that change-of-address card, a probate court clerk in the city of my birth called.

"Your father has died. He left you money in the form of Treasury notes and bonds."

"My mother and stepfather were right! Who would have thought that Midas was really sitting on a pot of gold?"

"Excuse me?" said the clerk. He had the mild, flat voice of the city of my youth.

"Nothing," I said. "Please continue."

"There's no will," the clerk continued. "The house will be sold by the city and the proceeds divided equally between your older brother, your younger brother, and you. You are the only son listed as beneficiary on the notes and bonds."

"There is no older brother," I said. "I have a younger half-brother. That's it. He may live in Florida. I think his name is Jerry."

"Yes, you have a younger brother in Florida. His name is Jerome. He was adopted by his stepfather when he was two. Apparently, you also have an older brother," the clerk said. "Our records show that your father was married briefly before he married your mother, and he and his first wife had a son, James. That marriage was annulled because it was so brief. James was adopted by his stepfather when he was three."

"Lorraine and Jerry don't matter," my father told me often, when I was young. That was another of his refrains. "You're my first son. You're my real son. I married your mother for love. You were the only son conceived in love." I shook my head like a dog shrugging off water and focused on the call.

"Briefly? How briefly?" I asked.

"Two weeks," the attorney said.

I laughed—a short bark.

"That sounds exactly like my father," I said. "I believe you. So he was rich and had four wives and three sons. What a great track record. Who would have guessed? What are the next steps? Tell me what I need to do regarding the bonds." Apparently, there was no stage of my life into which my father could not throw a wrench.

My wife and I redeemed the notes and bonds, and then wondered what to do with the money. Rather, she wondered and I brooded. The money wasn't enough for huge changes, but it could make our lives easier. While she dreamed and tried to talk to me, I spoke to James. He lived in a small town in the next state over from where I grew up and worked as a clerk in a feed store.

"I never knew you existed," I repeated into the phone.

"I never knew *you* existed," he said. "My mother never talked about that time. She only said that our father was handsome and that he got involved with her to make your mother jealous. Your mother was his girlfriend, and he wanted to marry her, but she kept breaking up with him. He married my mother to make your mother jealous enough to come back to him. "

"I guess it worked," I said.

"My mother married her high-school sweetheart," James continued, "and he adopted me, and they had three more children, and it all turned out OK. I consider him my father, and he considers me his son. He's in his eighties now and lives with my wife and me. I never wanted to meet my biological father, and he never tried to get in touch with me. I hope everything turned out OK for you, too."

"Yes, thank you," I said. "You'll be getting a check for a third of the house."

"Well, I don't feel I deserve it," he said, "but who am I to argue with the law? Thank you. It'll come in handy. My wife and I might take a vacation, and we will definitely help our son pay off his college loans." We said good-bye. James sounded nice. I was sorry when the call ended.

My wife continued to talk about her ideas for spending some of the money, and I pretended to listen.

"Let's move to a nicer house. Let's buy a cabin somewhere for a vacation home. Maybe we can take a trip to Europe? You could go back to school for a different degree. We could buy a better car. What do you think? What do you want?" I don't know what I thought. I don't know what I wanted. I just know what I did. I left a job with benefits that I liked well enough and took a minimum wage job that I despised and that didn't have benefits, so I could "help people."

"Why are you doing this?" my wife kept asking me. "Are you trying to prove that you're not your father? You are not your father! Where does this nonsense come from? Get some help! Talk to a therapist! Ask a doctor for medication! You're having a nervous breakdown, Danny! How does getting some money from the death of a selfish, crazy man you weren't in touch with for years have anything to do with helping strangers? He didn't help people! He didn't help you!" I heard her words from far away, even though she was standing next to me.

After a few months she stopped asking me questions and found a new job with benefits to cover both of us. She put most of the money from my father in the bank, where it sat unused, leisurely collecting interest, and with the rest she bought herself a cello, something she had always wanted. She began taking cello lessons, and every evening she practiced for at least an hour. I didn't mind.

I liked hearing the music. I had played the trumpet for a little while in elementary school, but my mother and stepfather wouldn't let me practice at home. They said the music interfered with their watching television. I was glad my wife had her cello and liked to play it. I heard the music as if from a great distance, but it still sounded lovely, like a world I dreamed of but couldn't enter.

I left my menial job for another menial job, and then another, until I ran out of jobs and the desire to find one. I wandered around town. I read books. I went to therapy. I got medicine. It helped a little, but not enough. A few years passed while my wife worked and played the cello and talked to me, and I listened not to her but to what the therapist said was anxiety and depression. I missed my wife. I missed myself. I missed us. My in-laws got old, then older, then incapable of living on their own. They moved to an assisted living facility and died soon after. I missed them too.

My wife moved out last fall.

"I tried," she said to me, one hand on the doorknob and the other holding the red suitcase she bought in college that still looked new because we never went anywhere. "I tried for so long. I'm moving out for a while. I found an apartment to rent, and I signed a lease for six months. We can see what's going on with you after six months. If things are better, I'll consider coming back. But things have to be better."

"I know you tried," I said. "You did everything right."

"You're residing in one life and living in another," she said. She sounded sad but not angry. Anger came, stayed, and went some months ago, like the summer thunderstorms of my childhood.

"I don't want to live like this anymore. I thought we could use the money from your father to be happier. But getting that money made you more unhappy than you already were. Right now I can't be here." She put her hand against my cheek. She closed the front door gently. I heard her car start up. It had that little hiccup in the ignition it always had, like a shy child holding back for a minute before blurting out the words. Neither of us had bought a new car with the money. We hadn't traveled. Only my wife and her cello were traveling, to a rental apartment on the other side of town, without me.

I stayed in the house. I'm still in the house. I'm old enough now to have Medicare and Social Security, so I no longer need to find a job with health insurance. When I was forty or fifty, that fact alone would have made me burst into song and dance. Most days I drink instant coffee and eat cold canned soup and beans. We stocked up during the pandemic. When I run out of clean clothes I do a laundry. I watch television. I try to read. I watch the leaves flutter and spin across the lawn and against the windows. Sometimes I sit on the deck and speak to my in-laws, even though they're dead.

"I miss you," I tell them. "Thank you for everything you gave us and everything you did for us." What comforts me most is remembering how Rosemary beat the odds. I don't know why thinking about that dead-baby-basket story calms me, but it does.

"Why do you think it calms you?" my therapist asks me. I still see her once every week or two.

"I don't know," I say. I think about it while she waits, looking at me. Rosemary was put aside for dead. She would have died if a nurse hadn't noticed her faint breaths and yelled for the doctor. But the nurse did yell, and the doctor did respond, and Rosemary survived. I like to think that she is still alive. I hope the widower she married is a wonderful man. I hope that every morning she pours chocolate chips into a bowl and eats as many as she wants, whenever and wherever she wants.

Now it's March. The days are windy. My wife moved out five months ago. A few perennials still come up in the garden we planted years ago, even though everything has mostly gone to seed. They surprise me now with small blazes of color. There is one wizened carrot that I admire before throwing it out, plus a few scruffy, straggly herbs—mostly basil, but others whose names I forgot or never knew. I can't remember what I planted, and my wife was annoyed because I mashed all the seeds together instead of keeping them separated, but the combined smells are familiar. I close my eyes and breathe them in, counting four breaths in and four breaths out. My therapist says that's called coherent breathing. Slowly, slowly. My life pulsates red and gold against my eyes. I am trying to come back. I breathe. In, two, three, four. Out, two, three, four. Repeat, repeat, repeat, repeat.

Album Leaf

On the last Saturday in June, Rose is driving to her fiftieth birthday party. Lucy, her daughter, has been planning this party for months. It's supposed to be a surprise, but Rose has long been aware of hushed telephone conversations and furtive glances. For weeks, crumpled paper has bloomed in the wastebaskets. Lucy asks insistent questions about food and friends while she watches Rose knead dough or chop vegetables.

"Do you like Italian or French food the best? Would you eat sushi? Do you like Janet better than Marsha?" Rose tells Lucy that she likes both Italian and French food, but the next morning, as she drives Lucy to school, she makes sure to mention that Heaven, a new restaurant several towns away, makes the best fries she's ever tasted. They are crisp on the outside and meltingly soft within. The generous portion comes with homemade ketchup. The smell of the ketchup brings tears to Rose's eyes. She doesn't know why. Rose knows her friends' husbands will appreciate Heaven's enormous steaks and burgers, and her friends will enjoy the chance to dress up and order blackened fish followed by a fattening dessert. The pastry chef is admired throughout the state for her elaborate, fanciful concoctions involving chocolate and heavy cream as well as deceptively simple yellow, coconut, and lemon layer cakes with buttercream frosting.

"Janet and Marsha are both good friends," Rose says to Lucy. "And I will never, ever eat sushi, and neither will your father." If Rose has to be the center of attention at an expensive meal for which Leo and she are paying, she wants to eat those fries and smell that ketchup. She is sure that the chef uses heirloom tomatoes to make it. There might be a little sugar in the ketchup, and some vinegar, and sweet onions that have simmered for a very long time.

It's almost seven, and the sun is unclenching its grip on the day. Rose cautiously merges onto the highway, turning up the radio so that she can hear the music over the wind.

"Our next piece is Mendelssohn's Album Leaf, Opus 117, in the key of E minor," says the announcer. "Mendelssohn wrote this piece in 1837, the year he married Cécile Jeanrenaud."

"Mendelssohn," says Rose idly. She knows the Songs Without Words, but she has never heard of Album Leaf. The brooding, stormy music begins. After several bars, the piano is already fortissimo. "What an unhappy piece to write during the first year of marriage," Rose thinks.

In addition to planning Rose's birthday party, Lucy has been planning her own wedding, despite the absence of a potential groom or even a boyfriend. Several nights ago, Rose listened to Lucy describe her latest wedding scenario. "I'm getting married on the beach in California. I'll invite three hundred guests, and I'll wear a long red silk dress but no shoes. My hair will be loose so it blows in the wind. I'll carry lots of flowers. After the ceremony, I'll fling the flowers into the ocean. And I'll tell the groom to go away."

"Why not give the flowers to the guests?" Rose asked, but Lucy just shook her head and smiled, as if Rose were being foolish. Rose knows that Lucy will be able to plan whatever sort of wedding she wants. She was always an organized and precise child. When she was small she asked Rose questions every day: "Do birds have knees? Why do golf balls have dimples? What is it called when your mind and your heart and your body are in the same place at the same time? Why is the sky blue? Is each snowflake different? How many horses are there in the world?"

"I could never plan a wedding," thinks Rose, as Album Leaf shifts to a major key but retains the same undulating rhythm.

As a quiet, lonely child Rose sketched out her life: a job in a library and two cats to keep her, and each other, company. When Rose turned six, her mother took her to get a library card and helped her pick six books—the maximum number allowed. Rose read them all that afternoon, then begged her mother to take her back to the library for six more books. Each day she asked for more books. The characters in books were safer than real people. You knew what they were thinking, even when they said or did the opposite, or said nothing at all. And yet, in her junior year in college, Rose looked at Mark, a senior, and fell in love with him the way a diver plunges off a bridge. Entwined with Mark on his narrow dormitory bed, his long arms wrapped around her, Rose cautiously and then with abandon redefined the contours of her life to include happiness.

Mark went off to law school after graduation, and Rose became a senior. She began applying to schools with graduate library programs in or near the city in which

Mark attended law school. They talked about renting an apartment together. When their year apart was almost over, Mark called Rose and told her it was over.

"I'm in love with someone else," he said calmly. Rose still remembers gripping the telephone and asking stunned questions. She doesn't remember hanging up the phone. She sat on the floor of her room, weeping. At the end of the summer, ten pounds lighter and still shaky, she found a studio apartment and a job as a library assistant at a law firm. She avoided her neighbors and let her friends from college drift away. Once a week, until her parents died, she ate dinner with them.

"He didn't deserve you, Rose," her father said once, but she didn't answer him. What was there to say? Returning to her solitary life was almost effortless. Chunks and edges of fiction still floated in her mind. When Rose shut her eyes, she saw the printed pages, word for word. She spent her weekdays in the library and her evenings reading at home. On weekends she cleaned, shopped, and did laundry. On Mondays, she returned to work.

Leo came to the law firm to do electrical work. Lights in the library had been flickering and sizzling for several weeks. He passed Rose's desk twice a day, each time saying hello.

"Hello," Rose would reply, meeting his eyes and then looking away. One afternoon he asked Rose to have dinner with him. They were both surprised when she agreed. At a Polish restaurant in a neighborhood where Rose had never been, they drank tea and ate dumplings stuffed with onions and cheese and crowned with sour cream. Rose felt oddly light, despite the heavy food.

"Goodnight," Leo said when they reached Rose's building. "I had a good time." He held out his hand. Rose took his hand and held it.

"Please don't leave," she said. Afterwards, they fell asleep on Rose's narrow bed, under the same blanket she had taken to college.

Leo's widowed mother, his two older brothers, and their wives were the only guests at the wedding. The brothers were portly, red-faced, and already sunk into middle age. One wife was thin and shrill; the other was fat and seemed kind. Rose looked at them and panicked. She wanted to turn around and run. Then Leo smiled at her and squeezed her hand.

Leo had thick blond hair then, with glints of reddish gold in his beard. Lucy has his golden hair. "What a beautiful girl!" people always say. After the wedding ceremony they ate Chinese food at a bright, noisy restaurant. The waiter gave Leo and Rose double handfuls of fortune cookies, and Leo gave him an enormous tip. When Rose became pregnant, they bought a small house. Every year Leo plants a vegetable garden.

"Look!" he says each summer, cradling plum tomatoes and green peppers in his shirt. When Lucy was small, he played board games with her every evening and took her to the park on weekends. They'd come home sweaty and flushed, lips and cheeks smeared with the lurid reds and blues of ice pops. Rose made friends for the first time since college, first because she needed to for Lucy, and then because she wanted to. Lucy has probably invited all of them and their husbands to the party.

Every few weeks the women meet for lunch. Last time, while they were finishing their coffee and dividing the check, one of them—was it Carla?—suggested that they rent a van and drive cross-country.

"For our fiftieth birthdays we'll find our old boyfriends who left us and sleep with them just once and then leave them in the dust!" she said.

"Does that mean we should sleep with your old boyfriends, or do we just wait for you to finish?" someone asked. Rose smiled. Her friends have begun to joke about the past. Daily they complain about their bodies, their husbands, and their lives. Rose resists complaining.

"I don't have anything to complain about," she says if they ask. When she looks at her naked body in the bathroom mirror, late at night, she is not displeased by what she sees. Does she see, or merely imagine, a twist of pity across her friends' faces? Are they wondering if anyone can have no complaints? The truth is, as much as Rose loves Leo, she has never stopped thinking about Mark. She does not want to share this fact with anyone.

The women check their watches and exclaim. They collect money for the bill and tip and exchange hugs and kisses. Groaning about the amount of food they have eaten and the need to resume dieting immediately, they rush off to meet school buses or drive to their children's soccer games.

"You're too thin, Rose!" someone always says as she brushes her lips against Rose's cheek. Rose always stays a little longer, by herself, finishing her coffee and taking a few more bites of her half-eaten sandwich or muffin. She only has Lucy; her friends all have two or three children. Leo and she talked about having a second child, but it never happened. Some of Rose's friends have jobs or do volunteer work. Rose stopped working years ago.

"Stay home," said Leo. "Read. Cook. Relax. Do something you have always wanted to do, like take music lessons." Her friends' lives are more frantic than hers.

"Have a great weekend!" they call to each other.

"We're going into the city to see a play," Marsha says.

"The kids are staying with my in-laws," says Janet. Rose and Leo will stay home. She rents movies for Leo and brings home books for herself. She'll cook a nice dinner, something that takes a lot of time, like lasagna with homemade noodles and Bolognese sauce from scratch. She'll wrap her arms around Leo as he dozes in front of the television. Last Saturday, when she kissed the top of his head, she noticed that his hair was thinning. When did the gold in his beard lose its luster and turn to gray? Before she met Mark, she could have lived alone forever. Now, she is not sure she ever can.

The middle section of Album Leaf ends, and the minor key resumes. The third section is the same as the first.

"Isn't the middle section supposed to be the stormy one?" thinks Rose as she exits the highway. When Lucy was born, Rose sent a birth announcement to the college newspaper. She wanted Mark to know that she was married and had a child. She always looked for news of him, but there was none. Last year, in the supermarket, she opened the brand of shampoo Mark used in college and breathed it in.

"Excuse me," people murmured as they steered their carts around her. Rose put the uncapped bottle back on the shelf, left her half-filled cart in the aisle, and went home to search for Mark. What did people do before computers? How simple it was to look for him at last.

How simple it was to find him online. He looks much the same, although silver smudges his once-black hair. He lives an hour away,. She wrote a cool, noncommittal email that he could easily ignore. He called the same day. After a few weeks of emails and phone calls, they agreed to meet. That was a year ago. They have met six times.

"This won't work if either of us gets greedy," Mark cautions. By "us," Rose knows he means her. There is always a difficult moment at the beginning. Rose takes a train; Mark comes from his office, unknotting his tie with his left hand as he pushes open the motel door with his right. Rose leans against him for several minutes while she swallows hard and blinks back tears. After she wipes her eyes and smiles, he looks at her intently before he leans down to kiss her. She thinks that he is giving her a chance to change her mind, because this is all that there will ever be. He will never leave his wife, and she will never have to decide if she would leave Leo. Each time, his level gaze asks her, "Do you agree that what happens in this room is enough?"

After the first time, Rose was so late getting home that she could only make something quick for dinner. She made an omelet, which made her think that the hotel bed was a griddle brushed with sun and Mark kept them pressed together no matter which way they turned. She couldn't stop kissing him, as if his mouth were an endless pitcher. With each drop, another year evaporated. With each kiss, every sound stalled and hushed outside the window. Their watches and wedding rings dozed placidly on the dresser. A double bed is so much nicer than a narrow dormitory bed, but everything else is the same.

Mark always gets up first and starts to dress. At the door he kisses Rose lightly—once, twice, again.

"When?" she says, her fingers tracing the perfect scroll of his lips.

"The month after next should work," he says. "If not, the month after that. I'll be in touch." He kisses Rose one last time, and she watches him leave. Then she showers and dresses and sits in the chair by the window, although she is already somewhere else—kissing Leo's head as he dozes in front of the television, in the dormitory hall cradling the telephone against her cheek and then her heart, fumbling with the buttons of Mark's starched shirts, holding newborn Lucy in a pink blanket, or sitting close to Leo in the Chinese restaurant, their hands with new gold rings clasped amidst the plates of meat and noodles. She is in all those places at once, and it makes her cry. It's the feeling she has when she smells the ketchup at Heaven. Perhaps there is a word for this feeling. Soon she will get dressed and take the train home. Lucy has a key, so there's no rush, but she likes to be home when Leo arrives.

Sometimes Rose still wants to ask Mark questions, ones that he will answer in his precise, thoughtful way:

"Do you ever wake up pinioned at the border of memory and desire?" "If you could do it all over again, would you choose me?" At first Rose sent Mark an avalanche of email about movies, books, and music.

"I'm too busy to write back often," he responded, "but please keep writing. I enjoy what you tell me." Lately, though, Rose feels that she is having a monologue. Picking her way through a conversation with Mark now seems like choosing what rock to step on in a slippery stream. Which one will hold her weight and let her advance? Which one looks fine but will make her slip and fall? How many times can she pick herself up without injury? She doesn't write him as often now. She doesn't tell him that she used to keep an empty frame on her desk, next to several of her favorite photographs of Leo and Lucy.

"It's an odd size," she explained to Leo when he asked why it was empty. "I'm waiting for exactly the right picture." A few weeks ago she trimmed an old photograph of Leo and put it in the frame.

As Rose pulls into Heaven's parking lot, Album Leaf ends. One high note is followed by several low notes that soften and fade away. The silence rings against the bright evening air. The announcer repeats the opus number. A cheerful Haydn sonata begins. Rose shuts off the radio and gets out of the car. She fluffs her hair with her fingers and slides her hands down the sides of her dress to smooth out the worst of the wrinkles. Maybe she has lost weight; her dress seems looser than it used to. Using the side mirror, she applies more lipstick. She smells her wrists to make sure her perfume is still apparent. Then she walks carefully to the front door of Heaven. She pushes the door open and prepares to look happy and surprised.

Inside Heaven, Rose pantomimes pleasure and amazement as she sees all her friends and their husbands. They have been seated in the nicest room—the room in back, with its view of the flower and herb gardens. White curtains billow, a soft breeze blows through the open windows, and the last filigrees of evening light glint on the tables.

"I didn't guess a thing!" Rose tells her daughter as she kisses her. Leo is smiling, and Lucy glows with delight. Leo and Rose exchange their customary look of pride over her head. Rose's friends look at her with affection.

"Nice dress!" one of them comments. Rose knows that she would not have gotten through her life without her friends. For a minute she thinks of her friends from college. Where are they? Do they ever think of her? She will always regret that she let them drift away. One called for years before finally giving up. Rose is determined not to lose these friends. She walks around the table, hugging each woman and putting her hand on each husband's shoulder. When she gets back to Leo she bends down and kisses him. This is Leo, who rescued her from sadness and solitude. This is Leo, who holds her without asking questions when she awakens in the night, her face wet with tears. "I love you," she says to him, and she does. But like a toddler who wants one kind of food when presented with another, it is not the life she imagined. That life was yanked away, like a cat rips wool from knitting needles. Rose wants that life, too. "I'm too greedy," she thinks. "I want too much, so I'll end up with nothing."

Rose slides into her seat at the head of the table, between Lucy and Leo. Her face feels flushed, and her heart is beating fast. Ignoring the glass of wine in front of her, Rose takes sips of ice water while everyone debates what to order and makes jokes about turning fifty. She reminds everyone that the fries at Heaven are wonderful.

"I heard the most beautiful piano piece by Mendelssohn on the way over," she whispers to Leo. "It was so incredibly gorgeous."

"Buy it," he whispers into her ear. "Buy all of Mendelssohn's pieces." She looks at him and smiles. She kisses his cheek. Her eyes fill with tears.

Rose tried her best to answer Lucy's questions. Some were easy. For others, she found books in the library.

"Birds do have knees, but you can't really see them because of the feathers," she told Lucy. "Golf balls have dimples to make the air cling to the ball, and then it travels further than it would have without the dimples. Look, you have a dimple in your right cheek, just like your father does. When your mind and your heart and your body are in the same place, that's called being alive. That's life. After you die, your body stays here but your mind and heart go somewhere else. No one knows exactly where. When sunlight mixes with the earth's atmosphere, the sky look blue to us. If you were an astronaut up in space, the sky would look black to you. There are more than sixty-five million horses in the world, and no, we are not getting one for our backyard, not even a pony. Yes, each snowflake is different. They all have six points, but each one is different." But now Rose thinks she should have said "love" instead of "life" to describe those moments when a person's heart and mind and body are in the same place.

When the food comes, the waiter puts an extra plate of fries and ketchup in front of Rose. "Your husband said it's your birthday and that you especially love our fries," he explains. Everyone quiets to eat and then resumes talking. Rose hears conversations about jobs, the news, and an upcoming vote on expanding the high school.

Then someone says, "A toast! A toast! Stand up, Rose, and make a toast!" The conversation stops, and everyone turns toward Rose. Is it her imagination, or do they look amused and indulgent? Are they wondering what she could have to say? "She was only ever in love with Leo," she imagines Marsha and Janet and Carla telling their husbands and each other. "Poor thing! She has no past." Rose stands up. She picks up her wineglass with her right hand and puts her left hand on Leo's shoulder. They are right; she has no idea what to say.

"Thank you all for being here tonight," she begins. She pauses, takes a sip of wine. "All of you are the loves of my life," she continues, looking first at Leo, then at Lucy, and then at each one of her friends. They nod and smile and wait for her to continue. Rose picks up a fry, dips it into ketchup, and slowly savors it, bite by bite. She thinks of Album Leaf--how the stormy section softened into calm, swung back into agitated melancholy, and then faded away. For a moment there is nothing but silence.

"Don't leave me, any of you," Rose thinks. She says, "I'm so happy to be here with all of you." She will repeat this sentence to herself every day: over cereal and milk, in the shower, in the car, and in the middle of the night, even when tears fill her eyes and she stuffs the corner of the sheet into her mouth or sobs in the circle of Leo's arms. She will say it so often that it will become true. For one instant, she thinks she smells the starch in Mark's crisp shirts and feels the small buttons under her fingers. His shirts are always white or blue. He is always unknotting his heavy tie with one hand as he pushes the motel door open with his other. Their watches doze forever on the dresser. The hands tick on. Sounds hush outside the window. The bed is a griddle drenched with sun. Rose shakes her head to dispel these images. She breathes in the smell of fries and ketchup, perfume, and evening air. When Mark calls again, she will try to say no. She will say no. She will try. She will say no. She will make one life—this life, her life—be enough. It will never be enough. She will try. She will keep trying. She will say no. She will try.

"Rose, don't cry! Why are you crying?" someone says.

"Oh, it's just the smell of these fries with the homemade ketchup," Rose says to her family and her friends to explain the tears overflowing from her eyes. She waves her hand in front of her face. Then Rose sits down and picks up her fork.

"It's nothing. Really, I'm fine. Please, please, go ahead and eat."

The Wanderer Fantasy

My dear friend,

These past years have been so very difficult, but today is moving day. After the Great Pandemic and subsequent elections, there were many calls for unity from politicians and others, but it did not seem that most people wanted unity. Things continued as they had been, with finger-pointing and harsh words, government gridlock, supply chain shortages, and outbursts of misinformation. At the same time, people continued to do what needed to be done: renewing driver's licenses and passports, going to school and work, scheduling repairs for cars and appliances, buying groceries, and following or avoiding the news. Vaccines became available, and the virus became yet another condition to be avoided or managed.

The country became more polarized until everything became a battleground. Then the envelopes arrived. Each contained a survey and a postage-paid return envelope. Everyone was required to complete the survey within five days and mail it back. The survey wasn't too long, and its purpose was straightforward: "Choose the country in which you want to live by answering the following questions." The country would be turned into two countries based on the survey results, and people would be taken to and resettled in one country or the other. We were told that details on what could be carried, what would be moved for us, and what must stay in our current location would be provided later. For now, we merely needed to fill out and return the survey. Survey questions included: What was important to us? Was it universal health care, or being able to make as much money as possible? Was it a lower salary and a social safety net, or a higher salary and lower taxes? Was it a smaller home and a pension someday, or a bigger home and stock options now? Do you plant flowers? How do you shop? What are the contents of your refrigerator and cupboards? If someone said or did X, would you do Y or Z or both or neither? If people did not complete the survey, they were mailed a reminder. After that, they were fined or imprisoned.

Months passed, during which additional letters arrived, with more information and instructions on what people could bring with them and where each person or family would live in their new location. Based on my answers to the survey, I was not surprised when I received my assignment to one of the two countries. I began the slow process of choosing what I could take with me and what I wanted sent later. Not for the first time I wished that I had chosen, or been chosen by, an instrument other than a concert grand piano, since I could not bring it with me. Still, at my age, even a cello would be hard for me to maneuver now. I hoped there would be a piano somewhere near my new home. If not, I would learn a new instrument or turn to another form of art.

Then, several weeks before everyone was scheduled to criss-cross the country in a web of buses and trains, with their papers and two suitcases and one backpack, I learned from a fellow artist that many of the surveys had been incorrectly tallied and processed, so that once everyone was resettled, there would be two battleground countries, not just one, and the entire relocation plan would be for naught.

"There's a third option," I was told. "It's a country for artists. Would you like to settle there?"

"Yes," I said. How could I refuse? Hadn't I spent my entire life looking for people like me?

And so I received my secret, separate set of instructions on where to go and what to say when I arrived. As soon as I finish writing this letter, I will head out to the meeting point. To one of my suitcases I will add some sheet music. After much thought about what piano music to take, usually in the middle of the night when I cannot sleep and roam the hills and valleys of memory, I chose, from a mix of composers, a prelude, a romance, a rhapsody, an intermezzo, a nocturne, an elegy, and a fantasy—the Wanderer Fantasy. It is not my favorite fantasy, but its name makes it an appropriate one. Aren't we all wanderers in a fantasy, looking for a place to call home?

I will leave this letter in the piano bench, on top of the rest of my music, for you to find, whoever you may be and whenever you arrive. I hope you, or someone you love, will be comforted by it. Until that day, take care, and be well.

Good-bye.

Library Book

Two children bring it to me. All the children here, and even some of the adults, think I have supernatural powers, but I'm just old. At first I tried to describe the past to the others, but they looked at me blankly. Without experience to pin a word to, what does that word really mean?

"Do you want this dirty old thing?" the girl asks.

"Yes, please," I say. She darts forward and puts it in my lap. The children never bring anything they find to their parents because they'll get punished for exploring. I thank the children, and they run off, giggling. I examine it. It smells musty. It journeyed through water and coffee or tea, which left stains. Parts are lost, and what remains is torn, crumpled, and hard to see. My eyes are weak, and of course there are no eyeglasses here, but when I squint, I can see two faint words on the battered spine: Library Book. I hold it for a very long time.

ABOUT THE AUTHOR

Ann Calandro is a writer, mixed media collage artist, and classical piano student. For many years she worked as a writer and copyeditor in medical publishing, medical communications, and pharmaceutical advertising. Her fiction, creative nonfiction, and poetry have been published in literary journals and anthologies. Her artwork has appeared in juried exhibits and literary journals. Shanti Arts Press published three children's books that she wrote and illustrated. Calandro, who was born and raised in New York City, received a master's degree in English from Washington University in St Louis. See her artwork at ann-calandro.pixels.com